Red Dust, White Snow

PAN HUITING

Fairlight Books

First published by Fairlight Books 2023

Fairlight Books
Summertown Pavilion, 18–24 Middle Way, Oxford, OX2 7LG

A CIP catalogue record for this book is available from the British Library.

1 2 3 4 5 6 7 8 9 10

ISBN 978-1-914148-40-8

www.fairlightbooks.com

Printed and bound in Great Britain

Designed by Wenjia Tang

紅
尘

Red Dust

I

The package placed outside her door was exceedingly ordinary – dull brown wrapping paper, no return address, no special logos or symbols of any kind to indicate where it could be from. That was what was odd about it – its almost *studied* unremarkableness in a world all about differentiating yourself. She was not expecting a parcel, having not bought anything online, at least not recently. She set the package on the kitchen table and looked at it. Other odd things became apparent. The brown paper was completely unmarked. If it had been delivered by the postal service, surely it would have borne some traces of its transit. It was then she realised the package had no stamp, confirming it had been hand-delivered. Who could have taken such trouble to do that? Who had been standing right outside her door? She checked the name on the package once more – it was hers, all right. She hesitated, wondering whether to unwrap it. It could be a bomb, anthrax spores, someone playing a prank on a poor woman in her late thirties living alone. Something would fly out the moment she opened the package, or an alarm would sound, scaring her.

After cycling through all the possibilities in her mind, she decided she would open it. She was too insignificant for anyone to bother eliminating and if it were a prank, her life would not be in danger. Even if she *were* to lose her life, well, there would be no one who would mourn. Her mother had died from lung cancer years ago. She had no father. She was an only child. The world would quite simply carry on. There would be a new girl at the office next week. Ideally fresh out of college, with long hair, full breasts in spite of her delicate frame. Someone, in other words, the CG artists at the company where she worked would want to grace the counter of their office. Someone out of their dreams.

She removed the wrapping paper to reveal a smooth, white, matte-laminated paperboard box with a cavity designed to hold the featureless white cube that now sat on her kitchen table – no bubble wrap or any other environmentally unfriendly cushioning material. She could see her humble kitchen reflected in the polished, mirror-like surfaces of the cube. It was as if a version of Kubrick's monolith had paid her a visitation. Any moment now, Ligeti's *Requiem* could be expected to play. She reached out to touch the cube. Just as her finger was about to make contact, it opened and a blue glow emanated from within. So fine was the seam running along the middle of the cube, bisecting it, that she had failed to detect it with her naked eye. Soundlessly, the top half separated from the bottom and *hovered* in the air just above it.

Wow.

Whoever had constructed this cube had spared no expense. Motion sensors, probably. *Levitation technology*. Impressive. Extremely.

There was a shallow round hollow on the surface of the bottom half of the cube and resting in it was a black disc about the size of her palm, made of the same highly polished, glassy material. She took the obsidian disc in her hand. It was cool to the touch and weighed almost nothing at all. Suddenly, the disc glowed to life, a message appearing on its surface, startling her so she almost dropped it.

Do you consent to enter into a parallel universe?

She paused.

She did not really believe the disc could transport her into a parallel universe; most likely, this was some kind of elaborate marketing campaign, one of those teasers you saw at the bus stops and subway stations that would slowly reveal itself in the weeks to come. Besides, she would be late for work if she did not get going. As she hesitated, the disc darkened, a lifeless piece of glass once more. Well, there would be time to examine it in greater detail after work. After a few moments of inactivity, the cube, too, stopped glowing and the top merged back with the bottom as noiselessly as before. She left the disc lying on the table.

Before leaving her flat, she pulled out her phone and logged into her Empi – short for Empirean – account. *Your gateway to life*, the company's familiar tagline, floated in white letters against a limitless ocean blue. Her avatar blinked prettily with eyelashes that budded, blossomed and scattered into a shower of petals. It had cost her, but she had decided to splurge on it because it gave her a discount on all her online shopping for the rest of the year, although the amount would likely be minuscule and the deal came with loads of fine print. After navigating to EmpiMaps in the app to check the bus arrival times – 'Never leave your house before consulting EmpiMaps!' went the jingle – she found out she still had nine minutes until the next bus. She did not even have to input the address. Empi already knew where she would be going at that time. She only needed two minutes to walk to the bus stop, three minutes to be safe, leaving six minutes to be filled.

Pulling out her dining chair again, she began browsing through EmpiGram. ianniechan had not uploaded any new pictures, which was normal, since the newest one was from two years ago, of his latest styrofoam sculpture consisting of uncut blocks – apparently, the oblong was his signature shape – laid out in an open lot somewhere in London. She could match the photo with the location on EmpiMaps of course, but it wasn't as if she could turn up there.

The arrangement might look haphazard, but it was supposed to call to mind a metropolis, or graveyard: 'the oscillation between two forms a statement against untrammelled capitalism', according to the caption.

By the time she made her way to the bus stop, the bus was just pulling in. Ten minutes later, she passed through the gantry of the train station and navigated her way through a sea of bowed heads, light and music from a commercial by a popular skincare brand invading her senses. Overhead, multiplied across the giant screens spaced at regular intervals, Aria frolicked among animated bees, sporting a striped black-and-yellow bob. Drops of light fell from the bees' stingers onto her face, shining, echoing a mountaintop transfiguration. Just a few nights ago, Aria had glided across her screen on rollerblades with waist-length, rhodochrosite-pink hair in a sportswear commercial produced roughly about the same time, something which her fellow human brand-ambassadors would not have been able to do, barring the use of wigs.

She worked for the 3D modelling company – Verge – that had created Aria: a virtual model, managed by a virtual human agency. 'Aria', an expellation of the caress between cheek and tongue – a soaring song, light as air, sending the subliminal signal that everything found on her was always desirable, ungraspable.

Clients were wary about using Aria at first. People want to see real clothes on real people, so the argument went, which turned out to be spurious. Since when had there not been an advertisement, a magazine spread or a photoshoot without digital enhancement? People knew that what they were seeing could not be real and instead the result of a whole range of tools and filters that *liquefied*, *warped* and *transformed*, but they wanted to see it anyway. In fact, they complained when all the pores had not been scrupulously removed – *slipshod work*. What they wanted was an armada of clones – the magnolia skin, the filled-up lips. Celebrities had to go under the knife in order to fulfil tastes that were getting increasingly... unreal, so to speak. Liquefaction was not so easily achieved in the physical world. When technology developed to a point where the integration of the actor's performance and the 3D models became seamless, it became a natural corollary to employ 3D characters in addition to the CGI backdrops that were already in widespread use by film and television productions. These virtual celebrities never grew old, never grew fat and always looked the part.

She had no hand in making the models at her company, though – they were churned out by the character modellers, who had to put up with the usual long hours and low pay, while the 3D characters they produced lined the pockets of others. Her function in the company was administrative – payments, invoices, that sort of thing.

There were a few others already there when she reached the office. Nick, from the animation department, slouched at his desk, his cup of black coffee placed strategically next to him. It must be near, within arm's reach, but not too near that it would be knocked over. She did not bother making eye contact, nor did she greet him. He did not look up from whatever he was doing either. They were all used to her ways by now. Nick did the rigging – something akin to placing controls and armatures on the character models, without which they would not be able to complete their hip-swaying walks or beguile with their come-hither smiles, leaving them as T-posed mannequins floating in 3D space, nailed to their invisible crucifixes. Kind of creepy, really. She wished people could see them now.

Jacq, who did mainly environments, had dragged two of her neighbours' chairs to supplement her own and was lying sprawled over them – one supporting her head and shoulders, the middle one supporting her buttocks, and the third positioned under her calves, while her feet stuck out over the edge of the seat. The only couch in the room was taken up by Alex. She forgot what he did. He was wearing the same hoodie he had on yesterday. They must have been working together on something that needed completing. She knew Verge had recently landed a huge project to produce a holographic installation for the developer of the smallest shoebox apartments to date. Aria was to finally cross the divide between the virtual and the real by coming to live in the show flat, waking up to her alarm, making muffins, keeping in touch with friends on Empi, meditating, learning new skills and engaging in creative DIY projects. Who said shoebox living was uncomfortable? Fans would be able to interact, ask questions and be treated to a house tour by Aria, thanks to proprietary natural language processing and machine learning technology.

The office filled up as it approached nine thirty. She munched on a breakfast bar from the box she kept at her desk. One by one they shuffled in through the front door, ignoring her and heading straight to their workstations, where they nodded or traded terse greetings. No high fives or jocularity yet. It was still too early for that and, besides, some of them were still unconscious. One or two took a detour to the pantry and procured themselves a cup of strong black coffee – the office's speciality. New recruits would quickly become indoctrinated; downing their first cup was an initiation of sorts into the fold. As for her, she kept to her own concoction with milk and sugar.

Paperwork occupied her all morning. At twelve sharp, she ceased what she was doing, picked up her purse and left the office. Lunch, she always took alone. Not once did she bring her food back to the office – she did not want to find herself in the same space as a colleague and be obliged to speak. She would, of course, when work demanded it. But in general, she kept interactions with her colleagues to a minimum. As time went by, if any of them needed clarifications about any administrative process, they preferred to consult each other before coming to her.

There was a time she used to go out, meeting people she got to know through Empi. But there was always something about these meetings that seemed incredibly bathetic. She wanted to drink the sky in a glass bottle – that was what the butterfly pea and coconut milk drink with stevia looked like on EmpiGram. But when she finally had the drink in front of her, instead of clouds, what she got looked more like the cloudy mixture you get in a water pot after a child's painting class. She was fascinated by the viral videos of bulging omelettes being sliced, springing open and blooming all over the plate, or cakes jiggling and wobbling in time to hypnotic music in the background. But it was like being infected by a food fantasy – all fantasm, tasteless when eaten. The truth is sauces congeal, soufflés sink, subject to the atrophy called reality.

Her dates also never looked as good as their images. She supposed they were similarly disappointed with her. In this tropical heat, make-up runs and hair gets undone. She felt ponderous, cumbrous, unlike the weightlessness in cyberspace. Words, once bandied about, sank like stones between them. She found herself becoming distracted by his collar, slightly curled. *Excuse me? What did you say again? I'm sorry but I drifted off for a moment.* Two times, three, and he would inevitably feel slighted. Conversation, already slowed to a trickle, would dry up at this point. *Thank you, I had a great time.* She imagined him entertaining his colleagues with stories about her. Or maybe, there was nothing to tell.

Lives on repeat. *Ad infinitum.*

'What do you do? As a senior officer in er... infocomms?'

'Many things.' A vague hand wave in the air.

'Such as?'

'Working with the relevant ministries, public agencies and industry partners to conceptualise and develop programmes aimed to achieve the desired outcomes. Obtaining the support and resources for them. Administering the funded programmes, managing the budget, tracking deliverables and outcomes, scheduling and conducting progress reviews... It's all to support the efforts to develop and communicate the vision and objectives for the council's initiatives in what they do.' A pause to check her reaction.

'So... what does a senior executive do in your department?'

'We assist in engaging internal and external stakeholders to understand leadership needs, co-ordinating with them so the relevant research and benchmarking studies can be conducted in a timely manner. You sure you want to hear this?'

'Uh-uh.' Always the collective pronoun, 'we'. Always 'assist', 'support'.

In the crush on the train, none of her dates tried to shield her from the other commuters with their bodies, all the while making sure not to touch her of course, even if it meant having to stand in a contorted position the whole way. The beaches they went to were always crowded and littered with plastic. People lounged on mats with their takeouts, while pigeons pecked at the disposable cutlery. The air seemed composed of cooking grease. She once saw a video of an oyster with a fine tracery of plastic veins – bright blue and car-paint red – threaded through its soft, squishy flesh. Too much plastic was being produced, it seemed; it was finding its way into food and water. Soon, humanity would be like that oyster – half-flesh, half-plastic, if it was not happening already. She wondered where the lovers on screen found their beaches in the city: places where there was never anybody else and they were always alone with each other, with no distractions. In a city that did not exist of course, except in a parallel universe.

She got honked by oncoming cars when they jaywalked. Her dates did not pull her towards them to save her life. She was not crushed against their chests. There was no charged, breathless instant when they gazed deeply into each other's eyes, their faces inches away from each other. Herein lies the eternal disappointment with human beings – they never behave the way you want them to. The beauty, of course, is when they finally choose to. But she was not going to take any more chances with that kind of beauty. Humanity was far too capricious and, for the most part, cruel; the moments of gentleness few and far between.

At six thirty, she tidied up and prepared to go home; not that there was much to tidy. Unlike the cluttered workstations of the artists, with references tacked to the walls, and books, figurines and all sorts of paraphernalia spilling all over their desks – quite a few of them were anime fans – her workspace was devoid of any personal character. For the artists, it was as much personalisation as wanting to bring a little piece of the world with them, within easy reach – like cave paintings, but with collage instead of ochre. As for her, she wanted her own effacement. She was just a sojourner at her workplace – that did not mean she wanted to leave her job; it just meant her workplace was not somewhere she associated her self, whatever that might be. She spied the animation department having a meeting in the conference room when she left, a blur of indistinct shapes through the frosted glass.

She did not join the mass evening exodus to the train station, but took a detour to the mall to pick up dinner. The checkout queue was long, filled with like-minded office workers wanting to stock up on groceries on the way home. She had a craving for instant ramen. Yakisoba dry noodles jumped out at her from the Gursky-esque supermarket shelves – except real life was never as saturated, nor as neatly arranged. Gursky's photographs were often stitched together from multiple shots. The *tour de force* ceiling was also missing – that had been the artist's addition.

By the time she got home, it was approaching nine o'clock. The disc was on her kitchen table just as she had left it, together with the cube and packaging that came with it. She was glad the ramen only took ten minutes to cook, including the time needed to boil the water. It even had a tab you could pull to reveal perforations in the lid to drain the water, leaving the noodles sufficiently dry. Talk about design. There were a dozen little packets to be ripped open and added, containing tar-like sauces and powders reminiscent of dandruff, but which conjured a wonderful aroma when combined. The whole experience was strangely addictive. Best of all, she could just dispose of the package after eating, without having to do the dishes.

The disc switched itself on the moment she picked it up.

Do you consent to enter into a parallel universe?

Parallel universes do not exist, save in the arts, popular culture and some highly contested branches of physics, but it would be great if she could escape this one.

Yes, she tapped.

You must agree to the terms and conditions.

I agree, she checked, scrolling immediately to the bottom. There was no use reading them. As with everything, she had to agree, or she could not use it.

Welcome to the parallel universe.

The disc went to sleep in her hand.

She sat at the table and blinked. Nothing else happened. Well, what was she expecting? The world to dissolve around her? A portal to materialise? Or her body to vanish where she was sitting, leaving no trace of herself behind? Feeling slightly foolish, she waved a hand at the cube and set the disc back into its hollow. It was a nifty gadget. She would keep it and maybe show it to someone, not that she had anybody to invite over. She stowed the cube away in the drawer of her nightstand, and disposed of the paperboard box and wrapping paper. She used to keep them, but they always accumulated faster than she could find alternative uses for.

After showering, she crawled into bed and logged into Empi while waiting for her partially blow-dried hair to finish drying. There was a drama on EmpiStream, *Love in the Snow*, that had the nation hooked, starring Josie Wong – or rather her double, since the actress had long since departed. A legendary name in Chinese cinema for her role as the beautiful fox spirit in *Miss Ren*, loosely based on the eponymous Tang dynasty tale thought to be the progenitor of the 'fox romance' genre. There had been many remakes of the film and many Miss Rens played by attractive actresses, but it was still Josie Wong's version that haunted with every melancholic dip of her lashes and woeful glance, making all her successors look like her distressed, wide-eyed ladies-in-waiting. Others apparently thought the same, for by and large every story with a female ghost or spirit of some kind would be made in her image. The performer behind Josie Wong's face was Helen Wu, who specialised in playing Josie Wong. No one could control Josie's face quite like Helen. If not done right, even Josie's simulacrum would sink into vapidity. Josie's puppeteer never emerged from behind the curtain. Most likely, it was a case of great irony – the name of a woman who launched a thousand ships, but not her face. If Helen Wu were beautiful, would she be content to live behind the face of another?

New episodes only aired on Saturdays and Sundays so the next episode was not yet out, but she could watch fan edits of choice moments from the drama – mostly centred around the male lead's face – to deal with the anticipation. She had considered starting on the series after all the episodes had aired, but she could not help wanting to be part of the online buzz, to leave comments under the videos. No one would read your comments if you left them after the drama had been screened. At Verge, she was content to let the stream of conversation flow around her, although there were a couple of times she contemplated wading in, silently composing her responses. Did she dare, did she dare, *senza tema d'infamia ti rispondo* – respond without fear of infamy? She pictured the eyes, hitherto unaware of being observed, suddenly turning to look at her and she felt unbearably exposed, ant-like, wriggling under a pin. Inevitably, she would wait too long and the stream would get diverted, leaving her behind on her atoll.

But now, she was content to submerge herself into the stream of data, feeling her consciousness fade as she dissolved into the solution of light and sound, letting it absolve her, until she was lost to herself.

Academy of Greatest Learning

2

She is perched on a rocky outcrop. All around her tower majestic cliffs lost in mist. The wind carries the terpenic fragrance of pine, reminding her of the room spray used by the cleaning company at the office. She feels like she is in a Fan Kuan painting – *Travellers Among Mountains and Streams*. The knotted forms of the trees, the hairline cascade glinting from a deep ravine on the cliff face, recall the seminal painting whose echoes are still resounding. A girl runs up, dressed in a white translucent robe over an inner garment of pale green, like layers of *qingbai* glaze. Her face is flushed, her straight fringe plastered to her forehead. Under those bangs, slightly upturned eyes stare at her.

What are you doing here? The Master is looking for you.

Master?

Her accoster looks like she has been running around all morning and is annoyed as a result. She realises she is also wearing the same clothes herself – a uniform of some kind?

Who are you? she blurts.

The girl's brows knit.

C'mon, this is no time to be joking around. The Master is getting impatient.

I won't go with you until you tell me who you are.

The girl rolls her eyes.

Ming Yu, she says with exaggerated slowness, in a show of great forbearance. Now hurry up!

Ming Yu (明玉), she repeats the name to herself, memorising it. *Brilliant Jade*. The girl is already bounding up the path.

Where are we going?

Brilliant Jade does not reply.

Ten minutes later, she is wheezing. Brilliant Jade must have spent her life in these mountains, whereas she is an unfit office worker. Some parts of the incline are so steep it is like a vertical wall in front of her. She begins to drop away from her guide, stopping to get her breath, but Brilliant Jade doubles back and tugs at her hand.

The academy's just ahead, don't stop now!

They crest a slope and finally she can lift her eyes away from her feet. Built right into the cliff face is the academy in question. She feels dizzy just looking up at it. Through an imposing vermillion gate that is clearly meant to be the architectural focus, she can make out a complex network of pavilions and gardens scattered precariously along the cliff. It makes her think of eagles' nests. Certainly, this academy does not look like it was built for humans – more like for bird-people. Emblazoned across the horizontal beam of the gateway are the words:

Academy of Greatest Learning.

What is she supposed to be learning here? No, why does she have to learn it? She assumes she is going to be learning something. After all, she is wearing a uniform, and she is going to meet a 'Master'. She feels Brilliant Jade push at the small of her back.

The only way to find out is to go forward.

Through mazey wanderings and labyrinthic passages Brilliant Jade leads her, and she despairs how she is ever going to find her way out again. Occasionally, she catches glimpses of rock gardens, lotus ponds and groves of flowering trees. Perhaps this is exactly the ploy: to befuddle her so she will be forever trapped here. As to why someone would want to do that is anyone's guess. Nothing makes sense to her so far.

Just as she is about to dig her heels in to stop their seemingly endless hurtle through shadowy passageways, Brilliant Jade stops in front of a door. She knocks. Three precise taps that reverberate through the wood everything seems to be made of. It is like being in the heart of a gigantic percussion instrument.

I've brought her here.

Without so much as a backward glance, Brilliant Jade turns on her heels and disappears. She would be in a hurry to leave, too, if she had spent all morning looking for herself, which she suspects is what Brilliant Jade did.

She contemplates whether to step in. She can still make a bolt for it – but where? She does not know this place. She can meet this 'Master', or she can spend the rest of her time hiding from everyone. Brilliant Jade was not exactly friendly, but she did not seem threatening or dangerous. She slides the door open.

Five crucibles burn in the middle of the stone-lined room, arranged in a ring around the eight trigrams on the floor, each crucible aglow with an astral light of a different colour. The one nearest to her is a vaporous black flame, flanked by a flame of thallium green on the right and a softly glowing white flame on the left. The crimson and yellow flames, no less luminous, are furthest away from her. The multicoloured fires light the room very strangely indeed. Many-hued shadows flit like ghosts around the room. The variances of light playing on the carved stonework make the surfaces seem almost opalescent.

A man steps into the centre of the eight trigrams. He is solidly built, more like a blacksmith than the alchemist you would expect from the merrily burning crucibles. He wears his long, colourless hair gathered neatly in a topknot, secured with a silver ornament. His long beard is similarly neatly trimmed and reaches his collarbones – *a good length for stroking*, she thinks. His robe, under the translucent overcoat of white that seems to be the attire of the academy, is pale blue instead of green.

My name is Zeno. Welcome to your first lesson in crafting. You know the five agents – wood, fire, earth, metal and water, he says as a statement rather than a question, stroking his beard. She has to suppress the violent giggle that threatens to erupt.

He has a surprisingly kindly demeanour. Judging from Brilliant Jade's attitude, she expected a difficult, irascible man. If he is irritated by her lateness, he shows no sign of it. She decides to play along.

So, Master Zeno... What am I supposed to be, er... crafting? She is not used to this manner of address.

Zeno... Zeno of Elea? The philosopher famous for his paradoxes?

Master Zeno clears his throat.

Summoning stones, he says.

She thinks she has misheard.

Summoning stones, he repeats. The sole purpose of your time here is to learn how to craft summoning stones in order to summon elemental spirits.

Oh dear, she thinks.

Let us begin, says Master Zeno.

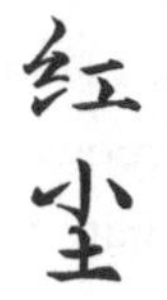

Red Dust

3

She woke to the sound of a rocket blasting off from the open car-park below.

Actually, a motorbike. But from the explosion, you would think it was a space explorer launching on an unfortunately long-term, recurrent mission. She happened to live in the blighted unit right above the motorcycle parking lots, although she really should not be complaining, since it was maternally bequeathed. The owner of the bike must do this on purpose, taking a perverse pleasure in adding to the misery of the residents drowsing under their covers, forcibly tearing them out of their cocoons – not that this protection from the waking world would last much longer. It never took more than a couple of seconds for the biker to tear out of the carpark, but it made waking up that much worse in the morning. It started about a year ago. At first, worming her way deeper into her pillow, she thought it was a one-off thing. But when it happened again the next day, and the next... She eventually dug out a pair of mini binoculars, the kind you would find in the National Day funpacks, for a good view of the top of the transgressor's head – male, Chinese, early thirties, dressed in the blue of an EmpiEats delivery man. She had written down his licence plate number.

She had no idea why she wanted to know what the motorist looked like, or why she had written down the number. She would not have use for either piece of information. She would not report him. She imagined the police casually hanging out at the void deck, trying to look inconspicuous, leaping out at the first roar of his engine. Would they do that? She doubted it. She would just have to endure her sonic prison, the way everything else was to be endured. One year later, the scrap of paper was still stuck to her wardrobe, glaring impotently at her, the once bright ink already beginning to fade.

Where did such a strange dream come from – toiling away with *Master Zeno*, trying to get her first summoning stone made? A creative variant of one of those dreams where you run all night trying to escape from something or someone, or struggle to finish an exam, or strive to find your way out of a wood, or a maze, or a building? A therapist would probably say the dream was a result of her battle with her feelings of entrapment, frustration or something of that ilk. The arrival of the cube with its mysterious invitation to a parallel universe probably incited her subconscious to take a trip into the fantastic realm.

She gathered herself and rolled out of bed, automatically reaching for her phone. It was her morning ritual to read EmpiNews or check her EmpiMail until she felt alive enough to make her way to the bathroom and start readying herself for work. Empi had updated itself in the night, so her avatar now sported water sleeves and had a cute new twirling animation. Upon tapping, she found out that today was the birthday of Xu Hui (徐慧), the world famous *Kun* opera singer who had performed in hallowed halls the likes of La Scala, Palais Garnier, the Met and the Royal Opera House.

Empirean's CEO Dismisses Privacy Protests as 'Unfounded'
#DeleteEmpi has garnered more than 1 million supporters, as activists raise concerns over the pervasiveness of the all-encompassing super-app.

Originally a messaging app, its functionality soon extended into virtually every area of our lives. First the social networking services, then the banks and the financial institutions. One by one, the operations that people rely on for the day-to-day running of their lives became subsumed under Empi.

Going somewhere? Tap EmpiMaps *in the app to plan your journey, book your ride share, your air tickets and your hotel, check out restaurant reviews and make your reservation. Want to know what's going on in the world? With its unsurpassed algorithms,* EmpiNews *knows exactly what you want and need to read, saving you the trouble of having to trawl the internet yourself. Why bother familiarising yourself with what's new on a dozen different websites, when you can get started now by using* EmpiPay *for all your bills, fines and taxes? Like the shade of lipstick someone is wearing on* EmpiGram*? Empi's image recognition is able to take colour balance into account and take you to its online shop on* EmpiBazaar*. All these, without ever exiting the app.*

With its unrestrained increase in font size, the article was beginning to read like a plug for Empi, which was only to be expected, she guessed.

'It's just easier to keep using Empi,' said a business owner. 'Everyone is already there. Why bother to go find your own customer base?'

But the integrated interface of Empi is precisely what makes it so insidious, according to protestors.

As one protestor puts it, 'When you do everything on one app, it allows for an unprecedented amount of data to be collected about you. The potential for exploitation is too great. We want a diversified ecosystem. No one entity should have all the information.'

Empi's chief executive, Ken Huang, dismissed these claims as 'unfounded'.

'The basis of Empi is trust. People are exclusively loyal to Empi, and not to thousands of other apps, because they trust us.'

Empi currently has 4 billion users worldwide, making it the most used app across the globe.

Unlike her Empi avatar, the eyes of the figure staring back at her in the mirror were red and puffy, rheum congealing at the corners. Her face was swollen, as if in rebellion against the sodium in the ramen she had – the result of an effusion of serous fluids into the cellular interstices, the tissue spaces, her body cavities during the night. A long moment passed. Two. The raw pink eyes stared back with the same displeasure. She lowered her face to the sink and proceeded with the ablutions that would make her look more like a human. How imperfect the body is, how *infirm*. She wondered how many people actually wished they could become their virtual selves, delivered from the intransigence of their flesh into the *unbearable lightness* of pixels, eyelashes exploding into a garden of flowers.

Thus washed, dressed, with human skin brushed on, she joined the human traffic into the heart of the city, with EmpiGram for diversion. It was Friday and she was already looking forward to the end of the day. She nearly dropped her phone when she saw what was on the new posts. After almost two years of silence, ianniechan had finally posted a new picture: not a sculpture, but a casual shot of himself holding a pint of beer, gazing at a spot off-camera. 'This Halloween I am a sci-fi character trapped in a dystopia of overconsumption on the brink of a mass extinction,' he wrote.

Because ianniechan so rarely posted, she was always afraid he might just one day delete his account. She had long made a copy of everything he had ever posted, just in case something like #DeleteEmpi ever happened and she lost her only connection to him. When she was thirteen, maybe fourteen, her mother had left her phone unlocked in the kitchen when she went to the bathroom. The screen was displaying the EmpiGram account of a man who looked like he was in his twenties, with the boyish, clean-cut features of an idol in a boy band. She first thought he was another one of her mother's students – many of them had that foppish look. She did not know what later made her search for him. Perhaps it was the audaciousness of a grown man – everyone is old to a teenager – using such a diminutive username. She would later find out 'chan' was actually his surname and not the cutesy Japanese suffix, and he was at least thirty-eight. He had been a studio technician at the Imperial College of Art, where he had graduated from the MA programme in Sculpture, at the same time when her mother was in the doctoral programme and gave birth to her, two Asians in London.

On application forms, her mother checked the 'Single' box, not 'Married', 'Divorced' or 'Widowed'. Over the years, he would recur on her mother's screens, as a tab on her laptop, on a window on her phone. There was no reason for her to think he was her father, but she just could not shake off the possibility. She became obsessed with him. Asking her mother directly was out of the question, not unless she wanted to trigger one of her mother's drinking moods. Staying on as a studio technician indicated he wanted to delay his entrance into society, to remain under the auspices of the college a little longer, but he left after just a year. It felt like he ran away.

He made sculptures out of styrofoam, huge blocky things that were mostly air, meant to be commentaries on superficiality, on artificiality. These filled up the space on his EmpiGram, at least in the first few years after graduation. After that, he mainly posed himself, caught in the act of working, looking grubby in the yard in a loose T-shirt that clung to his slender frame, or slouched over a workbench, a look of meditative concentration on his face. Only in one picture was he kissing a woman. She was not bad-looking, but next to him she appeared mousy, drab even, in her sensible clothes and nude make-up. Typical white-collar employee garb. Ian Chan, on the other hand, gave every impression of being too much of an individual to conform to any system, much less the nine to six. The lady was obviously the practical one in the relationship. She faced the camera, while his face was turned towards her to plant a chaste kiss on the side of her head. She looked overjoyed.

There was a latent buzz of activity in the air when she walked into the office – the clicks of the computer mouse were at a quicker tempo than usual, the gazes on the screens more fixed. The holographic installation project was in full swing. Her boss had messaged her with instructions to get interns on board to help tide them over. He did not call himself the director of the company he founded; instead, his name card read 'Dreamsculptor'. He also spelt his name as 'Jayson'. She had replied with a premium sticker of her avatar giving the thumbs-up sign with a wink. She would use the text she had always used, with some modifications – 'energetic & creative' would be changed to 'passionate & dynamic', for instance. The more tedious part would be to respond to the applicants: scheduling them for interviews if the project leader liked their portfolios, expressing regret in a professionally detached way if they had been rejected, or notifying them in a high-handedly congratulatory way if they had been shortlisted.

At twelve sharp, she left the office in order to beat the lunch crowd. Because she did not take her food back to the office and because she always went out alone, it was essential she went early so she could get a seat. When she returned, Nick and Jacq were still in the pantry. She considered taking her mug back to her desk and getting her coffee later.

'I checked: she got the *Flower Rain* lashes on her avatar, which give you a two per cent discount. Should I ask her to buy the phone for me and pay her back?' Jacq said.

'Please, it's *only* forty dollars. You're going to bother her just for that?'

'Forty dollars is still money!'

She stood outside as Jacq listed what she could do with forty dollars. Once again, she got the feeling of being poised before a stream. Did she dare leap in this time, or would the others laugh at her, in her red bathing suit? She had no red clothes. All her clothes were grey, navy and black. Fashion designer Vera Wang had called them 'Armani colours'.

I agree. An earned dollar is taxed – substantially. Better to save it. I don't mind lending my account. I gain the points, too.

Her colleagues did not exclude her deliberately, she knew. They were naturally closer to each other because of their work. She had become an administrator at a 3D modelling company because she knew people there would be just as enamoured as she was with simulacrums populating the space between self and the world. In many ways, the culture at Verge was indeed more accommodating to the unruly and the strange. In school, she never knew how to play games like bridge and Indian poker, cementing her position as spectator rather than participant. She never knew what to say and this made people around her feel awkward and uncomfortable. Rather than try to be appealing, she knew from a long time ago that it was easier to be of service, just as she was in her role of administrator. She might just be a cog in the firm, but a useful appendage nonetheless.

'We should do something, after this project is done.'

Nick had started a new topic.

'I-I don't mind.'

Who spoke? She did.

Silence pervaded the pantry. It was time for the disembodied voice to reveal herself, if she still wished for the genre to be *work-place* rather than *supernatural.*

'You want to watch *Hiryū no Yume* with us?' Jacq said finally.

'No.'

'Oh.'

'N-No, that's not what I mean.'

'Oh?'

'I mean, I don't mind helping you to buy the phone with my account.'

'Oh!'

'Let me know when you want to buy it.'

'Really? Actually, do you have time now? I have the link ready and everything. It's just a matter of making the purchase.'

'Sure, send it to me.'

'Thanks!'

When she left the pantry, she heard Jacq celebrating and Nick congratulating her. She imagined her pumping her fists in the air, eyes alight with excitement, the stuff of fancams. Jacq's doll-like features were definitely considered appealing according to society's standards of femininity – an exacting pageant you were born into whether you liked it or not – and she accentuated them by dressing like an anime character, wardrobe stocked with plaid and tartan.

The only other person she knew who put as much effort into her appearance was her own mother, who always dressed up, even at home, right down to powdering her face, and applying lipstick and false eyelashes. At first, she thought this put her mother in the mood for work – she was an academic and, when not at college, spent most of her time at home grading papers or working on whatever research she was occupied with at the time. Later, she suspected her mother viewed living itself as work. At the university where she taught, her mother stood out in her puff sleeves, bold cuts and graphic prints in a sea of equatorial cotton and dormitorial shorts preferred by the students. She made the institutional costumes of the other faculty members appear stodgy. Unlike the other mothers at the supermarket, she never looked like she had just stepped out from her living room. When she was younger, she had asked her mother if she was an actress, a question that seemed to please her. She remembered her mother's dresses even more than her person: those discarded moults slung over the back of a chair or on the side of the bed, suggestive of the vacated body of their owner.

When she got older, she started to resent her mother's outfits. They made her feel she was having consultations at her office even while at home; going to the same university where her mother taught only intensified the effect.

On the day of her graduation, she came home to find her mother sitting in the kitchen instead of in her room.

'I think,' her mother said, tipping her cigarette into the ashtray, 'it's time for you to move out.'

She remembered her mother's daffodil-yellow dress, like billowing sunshine, the only block of colour in the room that did not seem to be spinning out of control. She could not speak for some time. When she finally did, her voice came out in a croak.

'But where will I go?'

'You have savings, don't you? A week should be enough for you to find a place, since you've now nothing to do.'

She did have savings, they both knew. She went home as soon as her classes were over; aside from food and transport, she had nowhere to spend her allowance. She ate simply when she was alone. Unlike her mother, she had no interest in clothes, wearing the same food-stained hoodie to college and at home until her mother said, 'Oh for goodness' sake, throw that thing into the washing machine already!' She had never seen her mother lolling around in slacks. Maybe she did, after her daughter had moved out. When she entered the workforce, she stuck to clothes that did not need ironing. Her hair, she kept unvaryingly shoulder-length. Too short, and it would stick out in the morning; any longer would take more time to wash and dry.

Ironically, they spoke more once Empi became the way they stayed in touch. Her mother would even, on occasion, set her writing aside and come out to have a meal with her, like friends. Perhaps this removed connection was exactly what her mother was searching for when she holed herself up in her room, working on her research, leaving her to the care of the live-in nanny. She had four in total, who stayed on in multiples of two years, the duration of their work permits. The first two did not renew theirs, probably because she was a needy baby and toddler who cried a lot. The other two stayed for four years each. Once she was in secondary school, she grabbed her food on the way home and the nanny was dismissed. Later, when she came across the abstract of one of her mother's papers online – 'I/They Who Speak: Re-negotiating Personal Subjectivity and the Materiality of Culture and Society as Modes of Transcendence' – she would realise this was what her mother had chosen to devote her energies to: re-mapping, re-interrogating, re-imagining, re-situating, re-interpreting, re-positioning things such as gender, identity, power structures, spaces, bodies, narratives, sites of resistance, the self. She understood little of it then and not much more now. Her own degree was in Business and Management.

Her teacher had recommended she study humanities in college instead.

'You write thoughtful essays. You seem engaged with what we discussed in class.'

'Will I end up teaching?' she asked.

'That's not the only option. You can work in the civil service, marketing or administration.'

She knew a bit of what teaching entailed from watching her mother. Standing in front of a roomful of students was not what she wanted for herself. Since she would be going into the 'civil service, marketing or administration' anyway, it would be more practical to take Business and Management.

The weekend stretched out in front of her when she reached home. She had looked forward to Friday the whole week but when it was upon her, she realised what awaited her was another weekend with Empi, which was not that bad, actually, considering how well it knew her. She regretted not making the effort to pick up dinner on the way home. The milk and cereal looked unappetising. She had already consumed three quarters of the cereal and was getting sick of it. She opened the freezer and considered the abandoned boxes of ice cream, which were also sold in quantities too large for a single person and discounted only if she bought two. Cereal and ice cream – food that speaks most eloquently of isolation.

Academy of Greatest Learning

4

She is in a room lined with stone. On the floor is an immense carving of the eight trigrams, around which stand five crucibles burning with flames of black, green, red, yellow and white, in a clockwise direction. Kaleidoscopic shadows dance around the room, thrown by the iridescent light.

Wait – wasn't she here last night, in a tutorial of sorts, looking into the roiling depths of the furnaces, trying to discern their molten moods? Master Zeno had pointed out all sorts of steams, vapours, slags and sludges, showing her substances of mineral, plant and animal origins that altered the bubbling metallurgical processes, merging and interacting to awaken even more strange matter. But most importantly, he stressed that the art of crafting is really the art of cultivation of the heart. Rather than technical ingredients, it is what's *inside* the summoner that determines the outcome.

Come back tomorrow to retrieve your summoning stone, says Master Zeno.

Having a dream in the same setting for two nights in a row, and a sequel at that, is already quite a feat. She's not sure if she will be able to pull off the third night – if that is something even desirable. It points to an obsession with *summoning stones*, of all things.

She shifts her weight from one foot to the other, unsure of what to do next.

Ah, I forgot you're new here, Master Zeno says. I believe your buddy will be coming soon to fetch you, if you wait a bit.

What is a friend? A soul in two bodies, according to Aristotle. A rare occurrence in the real world but the *modus operandi* of dreams, where one's consciousness is scattered throughout every character. She helps Master Zeno to put away the used equipment, until they hear a knock on the door.

Enter, says Master Zeno.

The door slides open to reveal Brilliant Jade, framed by a rhombus of light from an unseen window. Her hair, under the light, is so black it emanates blue, like the finest ink of pine soot. She bows.

This is your timetable, Brilliant Jade says, thrusting a rolled bamboo scroll into her hands. We have the next class together. We have a bit of time, so I'll show you your living quarters before we go.

She is a bit taken aback by this brusque incarnation her soul has taken.

Take care of the new student, Master Zeno says.

They walk along the pebbled footpaths in silence. Normally, she'd be sweating, thinking of what to say. But this is a dream. These people are not real, but projections of her mind. What are the consequences of a botched dream? You wake up.

Have you been a student here for long? she asks.

One week.

That's not very long.

They walk in silence again. There are a hundred questions she could ask. *What is it like being a student here? Do you enjoy it? What class do we have later?* But she questions the need to get to know a figment of her imagination. As for the class they'll be attending, she'll know soon enough. Because there's no need to say anything to a fragment of herself, the silence isn't oppressive. The sound of far-off water, the gentle breeze rustling the leaves, and the chirping of birds and insects lull and pique her senses at the same time. It is soothing, yet many-layered enough to be interesting, like an artful ambient soundtrack drawing her in. She has lived with the hum and whir of machines and engines for so long that she has forgotten what it is like to hear without a perpetual, intervening drone.

They stop before a garden of raked white gravel flowing between rock formations. Overlooking the rock garden are twin verandahs. She takes in the low tiled roofs, the walls of wood and paper of the student accommodations. The architecture is simple, elegant – a scholar's dream of a retreat. Just as she's wondering who's the occupant of the room beside hers, Brilliant Jade speaks.

Your room is on the right, mine's on the left. I'm going in to pick up my things for our summoning class. You can take a look at your room. Meet out here in five minutes.

Summoning class?

Wait, what do I have to bring? she asks.

You don't have any summoning stones yet, right? Just attend the class for now.

The room is candlelit and a cosy nine feet square. A lacquer cabinet inlayed with a spring scene sits in the corner, together with a writing desk with a stationary box on it. There is also a canopied bed and a dressing stand with a bronze mirror. In the middle is a low table. The furnishings are spare, but not austere, an uncluttered space for thinking and musing.

She goes to the mirror to see how she looks in the green robes of the academy. Indigenous Chinese clothing has been gaining traction recently, with more people choosing to get married in it and fashion designers modifying it to make it more suitable for the contemporary. Some read supremacist agendas in the resurgence; others see it as a purely sartorial thing. Jacq, who has always been into dressing up, posted a photoshoot of herself on EmpiGram in a red dress with a train and sleeves reaching the floor.

She doesn't have Jacq's features, so any photoshoot of herself is more likely going to make the rounds on the internet as a meme. The only time she's ever going to wear a costume like this is in a dream.

When she sees the reflection in the mirror, she stills. The person staring back at her is *gorgeous*. It is undoubtedly her face, except everything she's unhappy about is gone. She traces her sharp jawline with her finger, her high nose bridge. Her forehead is rounded, her chin pointy. Her eyes are large and luminous. Her hair is a curtain of silk. She looks like one of the 3D models produced by her company. She disrobes and checks the rest of her body. Everything is taut; there is nothing slack or sagging. There are no traces of cellulite, no spider veins – just a smooth, unbroken expanse of lactescence most glorious.

She slumps backwards and holds onto the low table for support. Outside, Brilliant Jade calls.

Hey! Are you done yet? We're going to be late if we don't get going soon!

She goes out to meet Brilliant Jade, feeling like she's in a dream, which is exactly what this is.

What happened? You look like you've seen a ghost.

She did. A phantasmal image of herself.

As they walk, she notices how scenic every view of the academy is. Buildings are erected beside waterfalls, so lectures are always accompanied by the sound of softly tumbling water. Gardens are planted around wild ancient trees. Occasionally, they pass by other student accommodation built in pairs around a rock garden, like theirs, or around a pond with the autumnal reflections of maple trees shimmering across the surface.

They reach the rocky summoning field. The summoning class is taught by Master Xiao Chen (晓晨) – 晓 means daybreak, while 晨 means morning. Everything about Master Dawn seems to be sunwarmed: her name, her demeanour, her skin. She notices with a start a mole on the master's cheek that reminds her of her old teacher – the one who thought she would do well in humanities – whose visage flickers over Master Dawn's. A face swap from her past.

There are twelve students in the class. The picturesqueness of this world evidently extends to the people around her: everyone looks as though they could be a celebrity, with bee-stung lips, straight noses and chiselled jawlines. *Bee-stung* – the very adjective stings of torment, but in dreams, there is no pain.

Welcome, new students. The time has come for you to put your summoning stones to the test. For the sake of those here for the first time – Master Dawn casts her a warm glance – a summoning stone produces an instance of providence when the heavens, earth and man are in perfect alignment. I always believe the best way to understand something is to see it in action. Does anyone want to try summoning something?

She peeks at the summoning stone in Brilliant Jade's hand, about the size of a walnut and the peculiar yellow of canned creamed soup.

Are you going to try? she asks.

Brilliant Jade bites her lip.

I'll try, says a young man.

Brilliant Jade lets out an audible moan.

Qing Feng, says Master Dawn.

Qing Feng (青峰), whose name means 'green peak', produces a drawstring pouch from his sleeve. He empties a shower of stones the size of pumpkin seeds into his palm. She is impressed by how many he has managed to make. One by one, he tosses them into the air, but all disintegrate into powder, or vanish into trails of smoke, yielding their spirits suddenly, like the transmigration of so many souls. He is down to the last few grains now, disappointment becoming apparent on his face. Brilliant Jade has her eyes closed, as though praying.

Then suddenly, a white light.

The summoning stone disappears at the height of its arc but in its place, a shimmering tunnel opens. Out drops a worm, as thick as a forearm, with an anthropomorphic head on top of a white wriggling body. As she stares at the strange creature, Brilliant Jade shrieks and hides behind her.

Very good! Master Dawn nods. Will you be forming a contract with this one, too? Or will you let it go on its way?

I'll keep it, Green Peak says.

Why do you need so many of them? You already have two! Brilliant Jade wails.

Contract? she asks, patting Brilliant Jade's hand. Her buddy's fingernails are digging into her arm.

Summoning the elemental spirit is just the first step, Master Dawn explains. You still have to establish a contract for the spirit to serve you by fulfilling its condition.

Green Peak takes out a few scraps of meat that look like remnants of his lunch, which the annelid spirit attacks. Then, he brings out a sack, which the spirit enters.

So you just have to feed it? she asks.

Master Dawn laughs. These annelid spirits are in the midst of cultivation and still not fully sentient. As you become more adept at crafting, it's going to take much more to win over the spirits you encounter.

Now that the annelid spirit has been stowed, Brilliant Jade springs away from her. But as the class wears on and more worms are summoned, Brilliant Jade forsakes any dignity and shelters behind her throughout. No one else tries to establish a contract with the worms. She can't help but hide a smile.

It may just be a dream, but she supposes they have just become real buddies.

Red Dust

5

Her dreams lately were more eventful than her life, which could almost be encapsulated in a pocket-sized mobile device, which she grasped to ease her passage into the waking world. It being Saturday, she did not have to go to work but the rocket driver, the EmpiEats deliveryman, did. An arresting image of uniformed men ransacking the roadside shop of an elderly lady in ethnic dress drew her in, visual news specially formulated for the digital wall. She tapped on it, only to find other articles claiming it was a screenshot from a game. Café opening. An allegedly corrupt president claimed he had been misrepresented in an exposé documentary. His newsroom released the unedited two-hour interview from which his words had been taken out of context. Without embellishments, it was not as entertaining, so she skipped it. Signs of the next pandemic on the horizon. Signs of an economic recession. Man holding blank sheet of paper charged with unlawful assembly.

In the bathroom, she avoided looking at her reflection. After the gorgeous visage she saw in her dreams, having now to behold her flesh would be too much of a letdown. The flesh, as she recalled from an old Buddhist story of a monk who became attracted to a lady-in-waiting at the court, was overrated. He must have pursued her relentlessly, desperately, with many tear-stained missives of silk, his secret words bound with scarlet cords, for she finally consented to meet him.

It would have been autumn; a harvest moon would be illuminating the entire scene, which would take place in a rice field outside the walls of the city, so it could be carved onto lintels, painted in sutras. He would be excited, oh would he not be excited! Excitement would course through his veins like ichor, pooling at the root of his being, where it would swell and harden, tumescent. But surprise, surprise. Instead of a tryst, barebacked among the stalks heavy and drooping with grain, a formidable screen stood between them. His beloved had concealed herself from him. He would reach out, his hand trembling; was it a game she was playing or had something gone awry? The impassive silhouette held up an arresting hand, putting his advance to a halt. The latter then.

She proceeded to expose her body, but not in the way he thought she would. She exposed her body for the corruption it was. It was a sermon all right, but not in the *fearfully and wonderfully made* variety. This one was delivered in implacable, strident tones, like swords, bright white, through the heart. What he had desired so foolishly was nothing but a flesh-covered bag of muck and goo. The lubrications of sex? Slimy and gross. He heard the word *shit* come out of his beloved's mouth several times.

He was dumbfounded, *mortified* – in the double sense of the word. And then the *coup de grâce*, the final performance – she kicked the screen aside. Awash in moonlight, her white dress, her pale skin, seemed to *glow*. But this white dress was no virgin maiden's costume, far from it. Instead of accentuating his beloved's *innocence* and *purity*, it emphasised her *filth*. Her dress was stained with blood, pus, excrement and *Amitābha the Infinite Light* knows what. Her pallor, rather than reminding him of the magnolia flower blossoming in spring and emitting its heady perfume at night, called to mind a corpse. As for the nightly fragrance, why, the nauseating stench emanating from her body could only be described as *feculence*.

She stepped close. He dropped to his knees, retching. The vomit flowed out of his body, unstanchable. In order to achieve enlightenment, she had ceased to perform her daily ablutions, she intoned gravely, meditating on the vileness of the body in order to put to death physical desires. She extended a moist and sticky hand towards him, inviting him to join her.

*

After washing up, she went to the kitchen. What did Aria do in a room of her own? Painted her wall. Wrote poetry. Made a photogenic breakfast. The results posted on EmpiGram. She opened her own larder, regarded the box of cereal and closed it. Her room of one's own was closer to Beckett's than Woolf's, in which life plodded forward without anything happening. Unlike fiction, which skips over time when nothing happens, stasis and repetition have to be lived through in real life – the same job, the same rituals, day after day.

With pandemics being as cyclical as economic recessions, place had become virtual, with the physical often reduced to a bedroom. Spending the whole day indoors no longer carried the reproach of being a shut-in. Keeping in touch with friends virtually not only became socially sanctioned, but commended. She caught up with the happenings of ianniechan and her contacts, scrolling through their posts. Over the years she had amassed some 500 friends on Empi. Three had birthdays today – a secondary school classmate whom she had not seen since, well, secondary school; someone she met on an Empi game she stopped playing years ago; a friend from an Empi interest group on ancient Chinese dress – so she posted birthday greetings on their walls.

She had joined the interest group not so much because she was interested in the clothes, but rather for the photo manipulation.

The colours were edited so it looked like spring or autumn had descended on the tropical island, the flat equatorial sunlight modulated to pool endlessly in lambent courtyards and dappled gardens. She recognised the landmarks in the photos – the bonsai garden, the teahouse pavilion, the stone boat – all immersed in the otherworldly light that granted them a touching monumentality. The harsh tropical sunlight had made the Suzhou-style architecture look like cardboard imitations, like the wrong lighting had been used on a film set. One tourist video on EmpiStream even joked that the temperature was so punishing, the phone overheated and stopped recording.

Ever since she joined the interest group, she received news, ads and notifications related to traditional culture – from traditional music classes to historical drama trailers. She watched quite a few, which inspired Empi to send her even more.

The imperial harem survival game she played was also on the recommendations list. Die Ying (蝶影) or 'Butterfly Shadow', to whom she had just wished a happy birthday, was a fellow player on the online community for discussing game strategies. After participating in several palace wars together, they began chatting and she realised that Butterfly Shadow was a Singaporean living in Sydney. They spent many hours talking, sometimes through the night, while playing the game. She ended up knowing a lot – how she ended up there, her work, her boyfriend, a stalking incident in her childhood where the pervert would lie in wait for her at the void deck with his genitals exposed – and also nothing about Butterfly Shadow. This went on for about a year until she started logging in less and less. She did not know if Butterfly Shadow was still playing the game but the reasons to talk evaporated once she left. Apart from the game, nothing in their lives intersected. If she were to write a novel about her life, it would be a novel with no side characters. The fleeting thoughts and feelings constituting a character's stream of consciousness would instead be occupied by a steady stream of digital stimulation.

When she next looked up, it was almost noon. Nothing beats Empi at being a time killer. With Empi, one is never truly alone, except when asleep.

She made her way downstairs to grab lunch. On opening the door, she saw the old lady who had been living in the unit across ever since she could remember tending to her potted plants. When her mother died and she moved back to the house, she had been struck by the sight of the snake plants, money plants, spider plants, aloes and monsteras in their dragon motif pots, identical from her childhood. If not for her neighbour's greyer head, she would have thought she had never left, but merely pressed pause. The fact her mother died suddenly – a chest X-ray for a persistent cough turned out to be stage 4 cancer – had added to the hallucinatory quality of the homecoming.

'How's your mother? I haven't seen her for a long time,' said the old lady, smiling and revealing her blackened teeth.

It was important to smile to appear civil, but not directly at the woman so the cordiality would glance off into the distance. She used to reply that her mother had passed away but stopped when she realised her neighbour would never remember. She still did not know the old lady's name. 'Auntie' had sufficed in all their interactions so far.

On the ground floor, the gardens became more elaborate. She walked past swings, patio tables, red-whiskered bulbuls and merboks prized for their songs hanging from the sheltered walkways, as well as aquariums, decorations of windmills and fairy lights, profusions of fruit trees and rows of vegetables. There was even a flock of idiosyncratic duck-shaped garden statues that looked quite realistic at night. She suspected they were against the rules, but as long as no one complained and there was no dengue threat, the town councils were mostly happy to let residents sort things out among themselves. Some extraordinary jungle homes even made the news – the only window or corridor that was an unruly tangle of vines, foliage and creepers in the block's façade.

Although it was still early, there was already a queue in front of the economy rice stall. Not because the food was particularly good, but because the elderly man would carefully arrange every dish you ordered in the takeout box. Instead of picking your dishes one by one, he would request you order everything at one go so he could plan how each dish went into the styrofoam container. For some people, the slow service discouraged sales, but she continued to buy from the stall because she liked opening the box to reveal the neatly arranged contents. It made her feel cared for, even though she knew the stall owner's behaviour was more likely driven by his own compulsion than any special concern for his customers. As she waited, Alex shared an article on his EmpiGram with the caption, 'If I ever join #DeleteEmpi, this will be the reason', which prompted Nick to comment almost immediately, 'What?? Please... noooo!'

Why We Should Pay Attention to #DeleteEmpi

#DeleteEmpi hardly raised a peep in our city-state, which is not surprising, since protest is not usually the way people express themselves here. I'm not against Empi. I'm an Empi user myself. But even if we're not going to delete Empi, we should know at least what's being contested, because we're all part of this maelstrom, whether we're aware of it or not.

I am the person who made headlines when an anonymous bystander recorded my 'homophobic' and 'racist' conversation with my fiancé and uploaded it on EmpiGram. The post went viral and my privacy flew out of the window at the same time. My face was just another image Empi recognised, the same algorithm that allows you to search for the address of the place in a video, or the product you wanted to buy. When people found out I was a secondary school teacher, there were calls that I make a public apology, and even more calls for my dismissal. People continued to share my photos and articles because my viral status meant my humiliation became something people could profit off. Content that would remain searchable, always.

Yes, Empi is not the problem, it's the people using the technology. But we need to question where this technology leads and if it's where we want to go. 'Your gateway to life' is an exhilarating promise, a promise that all of life can be searched and indexed and served up to you by Empi. But how much of your privacy are you willing to give up for that convenience?

We need to ask if it's ourselves we're really devouring.

The original article had got many likes. But it had also got comments like 'Where's she working now?'; 'Did she get married to her fiancé?'; 'Why are you posting if you don't want the attention?'

At home, her robot vacuum-cum-mop cleaned the floor and made floor plans of her house to be sold, so she could continue browsing Empi. She knew all that was said was true, that every time she offered up her face in an Empi app for the momentary pleasure of seeing it superimposed on an iconic scene, or let the app record her voice to sing in an online karaoke room with Empi users from all over the world, she was giving up yet another piece of herself as data to be analysed and sold.

All that was commonplace. And yet.

She continued to succumb to the seductions of a frictionless machine world, of people kept at bay behind a digital wall, of the conveniences of an app that paid more attention to her than she did herself, even if the lubrication was a trap, a nepenthe that promised escape from time, from self, while concealing a slippery tumble into a gaping mouth underneath.

At six thirty, Empi started showing her food-related ads and she found herself braving the weekend queue at the supermarket to pick up a *lazy instant hot pot*. Besides, she needed something else to eat other than cereal and ice cream.

The self-heating hot pot came with disposable cutlery, wet wipes and toothpicks. Instead of freeze-dried ingredients, it contained slices of beef, tripe, lotus root, potato, bamboo shoot, kelp and wood ear fungus – all to be warmed up using the heat pack provided. Truly, the Rolls-Royce of convenience food, with a price tag to match.

As she checked out other dramas while waiting impatiently for the new episode of *Love in the Snow* to air, she received a reply from her secondary school friend.

Hey! Thanks for the birthday greeting! How have you been? Do you remember Estelle? It happens she's holding our first-ever class reunion at her place tomorrow. I didn't see you in the group chat so I thought maybe you haven't heard about it. Would you be free to come?

Her first instinct was to decline. But as she was making her polite refusal, she thought, *Why not?* Here was a proposal that would not have been made if not for the intervening years. She could not imagine being invited to any party as a teenager. Perhaps… just perhaps, one of her old classmates might even end up as a *buddy*.

Hi Jerome! I can't believe we're actually going to meet after all these years! Of course I'll come. Is it possible to add me to the group chat? I'm good... working at Verge. How are your wife and kids?

The reply was almost instantaneous.

Added! Wow... Verge!! My wife follows Aria on EmpiGram! Are you a designer now? My wife and kids will be at the gathering so you can meet them.

She had liked Jerome's family pictures on Empi without ever expecting to see them in real life.

Nah, I'm in admin. Looking forward to meeting them!!

Jerome liked her message without replying anything new, bringing the conversation to a close. In the group chat, everyone welcomed her like an old friend, their memories of her taking her recess alone seemingly erased by the passage of time. They laughed over photos of their teenage selves, retouched by the cosmetics of time; looking back, everyone was just as awkward – and beautiful – as the others.

It was way past airtime when she finally got down to streaming *Love in the Snow*. With dismay, she watched the timeline advance inexorably to the nail-biting cliffhanger. *A silver glint of a dagger, concealed within the folds of a cloak. Josie Wong's eyes squeezing shut, except the thrust does not come – the hero has positioned himself between her and the assailant. He lifts a trembling hand. It comes away red. Mournful vocals creep in. You are my destiny. A destiny like the fallen snow. The frame freezes on a split screen of their faces – Josie's stricken, the hero's pale and gasping, the antagonist's pulled into a triumphant rictus. The music swells to a crescendo. I love you. I love you. I love you.* She tapped on the

'Next Episode' button, although she knew there would be nothing there. Sure enough – *Not Available! The Next Episode Will Air Tomorrow at 8pm.*

A cliffhanger that never fails to work, no matter how many times it is used, even though there is almost no chance for the hero not to make it. Perhaps what is keeping the – mostly female – viewers' attention trained on the screen is the more open-ended question of 'What's to become of him?' rather than the yes-no 'Will he live?'

Kim Yu-mi's voice gives me the chills each time, she typed, enjoying the effect of the *Spotlight* accessory which made other avatars throw flowers in her path as she walked in. *Who knew 'I love you' x3 can make me miss someone I haven't even met.*

Her comment generated replies immediately.

Me too, said nana202.

Omg sis, saaaame, said j_e_n.

She spent another hour or so exchanging remarks with her brothers and sisters, the assenting lines of text accumulating like salve, transforming into a susurrant chorus in her head, lulling her to sleep.

Academy of Greatest Learning
6

After their summoning class, they make their way to a high-ceilinged dining hall with a long table down its length for dinner. The *dougong* is one of the most intricate she has ever seen – the interlocking roof brackets are carved from wood of different hues to create the impression of auspicious five-coloured clouds floating overhead. A line of students is already queuing before the serving station, where a row of cooks are ladling and setting food on the students' trays. Green Peak does not join the queue, but takes a seat at the table. She follows Brilliant Jade, who takes note of where he sits and chooses a place furthest away from him.

The menu consists of autumnal dishes, including a soup of snow fungus boiled with apple and pork, braised crucian carp, rice, fruit and vegetables. It is better than what she feeds herself on most days. She digs in, but notices Brilliant Jade sneaking glances at Green Peak every now and then.

Green Peak brings up his sack and releases not one, but *three* annelid spirits onto the table. Down its length they wriggle. She holds her sleeve in front of Brilliant Jade to shield her from the sight of their bobbing heads and wandering foetal eyes. Once they reach the edge of the table, they flop down onto the floor. Two worms balance a lacquer tray between them on their heads and join the dwindling line at the serving station, while the third worm fetches a teapot by looping its head through the handle and slinging it around its long neck. The teapot worm, which she recognises to be the newest addition from the liver-coloured mark on its tail, takes the teapot to the server standing by the vat of boiling water, who unslings it from its neck and fills it.

Tasks accomplished, the worms return, leaping onto the table. The tray remains supernaturally level throughout the acrobatics. She resists the urge to clap. Once more, they traverse down the table, a demented procession out of the nuttier depths of the subconscious; she raises her sleeve again when they come close, as if in salute. Brilliant Jade cowers. The worms tangle and tumble at Green Peak's feet throughout the meal. Occasionally, Green Peak will throw them some food, sending them into a frenzy. Brilliant Jade explodes.

Will you please stop that? It's so disgusting!

Green Peak looks up from his worms at Brilliant Jade, as though noticing her for the first time, winking as she scowls at him.

After dinner, most of the male students go for a dip in the springs, while the rest content themselves with the open-air tubs outside their dorms, under the canopies of cypress trees, at the end of corridors redolent of moss and leaves. She lets Brilliant Jade have her bath first, before taking her turn in the tub. Everything seems hallucinatory. The vitreous air. The moon floating on water. Is this why people go on vacations? In the past, she just allowed her unused annual leave to be forfeited, until she realised the joy of taking the morning off so she could binge-watch a drama the night before or avoid the rush-hour crush as the population inched closer to the 10 million target. She has no one to go on vacations with. Besides, the idea of waking up in an unfamiliar place, having to deal with all the situations that arise because you do not know the culture and the language, feels stressful to her.

After her bath, she finds Brilliant Jade waiting for her on her verandah with a bottle of plum wine.

This is brewed here at the academy, says Brilliant Jade, waving the bottle. It's perfect for celebrating your joining the academy, don't you think?

As Brilliant Jade moans about worms and Green Peak, she thinks how this is the first time she has had anyone over, and the wine feels exceedingly heady and sweet.

She wakes up early the next morning. Brilliant Jade spies her in the garden and sticks her head out of the window.

Where are you going? It's still early for breakfast.

I'm going to pick up my summoning stone from Master Zeno. The name now rolls off her tongue.

Hang on. I'm coming with you.

She kicks a pebble around as she waits, trying to suppress her glee. Not only has she experienced a slumber party – a party in her slumber – she now has someone to walk with. Never in her dreams would she have thought it could be possible. Until now.

Dawn at the academy is scented with dew-drenched verdure. As Brilliant Jade chatters by her side, she wonders again at how divergent her alter ego is, for she has never been loquacious. There must be depths to her psyche she is unaware of. She anticipates the kind of stone that will surface in the crucible. Will it be cloudy yellow like Brilliant Jade's? Or granular like Green Peak's?

There's nothing when Master Zeno opens the crucible.

She rubs her eyes, hoping to find a speck, if not a seed.

The stone disintegrated because it was not stable enough, says Master Zeno. It's quite common for students to fail the first time.

We can collect ingredients and try again after our theory class, Brilliant Jade consoles.

Did you manage to get anything the first time? she asks her friend.

Does it count if it disappeared before I could take it to the summoning class? It was a weird one. Some crystal with *a plume of smoke* attached.

The theory class at the academy is taught by Master Xiao Yun (霄云). Both characters in her name mean 'cloud'. Master Cloud revised and updated *The Book of Elemental Spirits*, a classic written by Chao Ying (朝英), the first principal and one of the founders of the academy. 朝 means 'dynasty' and 英 'great talent'. Taken together, it could mean 'great talent of the era' – very appropriate for someone with her achievements. *The Book of Elemental Spirits* is practically *the* manual for summoners. It is a theory book, historical text and spiritiary all rolled into one. The spiritiary part is continually expanding, as more people add to it over the years.

Excerpt from The Book of Elemental Spirits *by Chao Ying, revised and updated with a foreword by Xiao Yun, 17th edition.*

Although elemental spirits may take human form, their true forms can be all manner of animal, fish, bird and every living thing that moves or creeping thing that creeps. According to the Pact made between elemental spirits and humans during the War, elemental spirits can be summoned by humans using elemental stones. The crafting of elemental stones will affect the type of elemental spirits summoned – a fire stone crafted in a fire crucible will summon a fire spirit; a water stone crafted with a water crucible will summon a water spirit, and so forth. By varying the composition of the elemental stones, different spirits may be summoned. For example, the addition of water collected from the Mysterious Spring that flows eastwards from the Ligustrum Sinense Mountains to a water stone will lure the Whirlpool Turtle with its gallinaceous head and ophidian tail. Its cries, which are like the sound of wood being split, have the power to unstop deaf ears. Resting your feet on its shell is also known to be an effective treatment for calluses. If you venture 300 li further east from here, you will come to the Verdant Knoll: its sun-facing side has an abundance of white jade, while its shadow-facing side an abundance of celadonite. It is the home of the extremely savage, man-eating Nine-Tailed Fox, whose cries are like a human baby's. Very much sought after for the immunity it grants to demonic poisons, it may be summoned if you add white jade mined from the sun-facing side of the Knoll and celadonite from the shadow-facing side in the ratio of 1:3 to your fire stone. The Verdant Knoll is also the source of the Fragrant Waters, which flows south, emptying into Birdwing Marsh, so called because its shape resembles a bird's wing. If you can resist the temptation of the Waters to drink it, it can be used to summon Guan Guan (灌灌), a pigeon-like bird with the ability to cure confusion, whose cries are like clamorous squabbling, when added to an earth stone.

The paragraph continues in this vein for the next ten pages. In her opinion, Grandmaster Chao Ying is too desultory and rambling. She also seems to be very much concerned with the cries the spirits make. Master Cloud, stern and serious, with the accoutrements to match – tight bun, glasses with chain – idolises her.

The first summoner, says Master Cloud, her blue robes swishing as she strides down the aisle, was a *woman*. She founded this academy, together with the Ice Dragon, and became its first principal after the conclusion of the War Against Demons. Our first principal was a *woman*.

Master Cloud has a strange way of inflecting the word 'woman' that draws attention to it, and she uses the word 'woman' often. She also speaks the Grandmaster's name with a breathy sigh. If she were Master Cloud, she'd not be so fastidious about preserving the Grandmaster's *voice* and would tidy up her prose a bit more. Stream of consciousness writing, though much venerated in fiction, is surely not the ideal form for a textbook. She would also put all the summoning stone formulas in a separate section, to improve readability and to facilitate future reference.

Needless to say, the more powerful the spirit is, the rarer it is and the harder it is to summon. There are many one-tailed foxes whose dens are all over the land, but to become a Nine-Tailed Fox requires millennia of cultivation. The way to the Verdant Knoll where they make their abode is arduous and fraught with peril, and the Knoll itself is enshrouded with a strange spiritual energy forbidding to trespassing humans. Powerful, ancient spirits are naturally averse to doing the bidding of humans. Many have chosen not to reveal the secret of their summoning. When the Demonic Realm sought to make the human and spirit worlds their own and waged war upon us, the Nine-Tailed Foxes allied themselves with humans to repel the common enemy. After the War, however, they retreated to the Verdant Knoll and were never seen again.

Foremost in the elemental spirit realm are the five Dragon Gods with mastery over the elements. The white dragon, Xue Long (雪龙), controls ice. Chi Long (赤龙) is the red dragon and he wields the power of fire. Qing Long (青龙), the green dragon, has dominion over wood. The golden dragon is Jin Long (金龙) and he commands earth. Finally, the yellow dragon, Huang Long (黄龙), exercises influence over metal. With the strength the dragons possess, it is unlikely there can be any energy net conjured by a summoning stone strong enough to hold them. The White Dragon was wandering south from the Forest Bathed in

Snow when he met me on a mountain trail. I was frozen to the spot as he descended from the sky, his snow-white robes billowing around him.

'What's this din that has roused me from my sleep?' he asked, his expression cold and his voice glacier. He was none too pleased.

'Wh-what din are you talking about?' I stammered, uncomprehending.

'Babies wailing. Infernal howling. Screaming, crying, caterwauling.'

I still had no idea what he was talking about. But the word 'infernal' made me think perhaps he was complaining about the demons. They were everywhere by then and it was not safe to be out in the mountains alone. In fact, I was worried I might be conversing with one. However, he had not made any moves to eat me. Not a demon then, *I decided.* An elemental spirit perhaps?

'Sir, I've no idea what you're referring to. Are you perchance an elemental spirit who is aiding us in fighting the demons and has lost his way?'

At my words, his expression grew thoughtful. 'Demons…' Then, piecing together all the information from the sentence I had just spoken, he said, 'I see, so spirits have decided to stand with humans.' Looking at me, he said, 'Have you been taught the secrets of summoning?'

'There are a few of us who are able—' I began.

He silenced me with an impatient flick of his sleeve. 'This is no good. Too inefficient. That's why this blasted war is taking so long. Nobody knows what they're doing.' He rolled his eyes. 'As usual.'

He pointed at me. 'You.'

'Y-yes?'

'I will start a school to teach humans the art of summoning. You shall be its first principal.'

So the first summoner is not exactly Chao Ying, but she may as well be the first one who was of any real effectiveness. There were 'a few', as the Grandmaster said, who had probably been rudimentarily inducted out of expediency. However, she knows better than to take this up with Master Cloud.

The ability to summon elemental spirits allowed contracts to be made, says Master Cloud, paving the way for a more reliable method to harness the spirits' abilities. Summoners no longer need to rely upon chance encounters and verbal negotiations to achieve cooperation with the spirits. Here she pauses to rap sharply on the desk of a student dozing off. Obscure ingredients posed no problems for the Ice Dragon, Master Cloud continues, who was able to traverse dimensions and obtain them easily. With the Dragon God in command, many elemental spirits gave themselves over to the cause. Once an army of summoners had been assembled and trained at the academy, the War ended within six days.

At these words, she can't help but furrow her brows. She knows of another war that ended within six days, after the bombing of Hiroshima and Nagasaki. *Fat Man* and *Little Boy* – what jocular names, puerile even; they could be the title of a comedy. Wars with a capital 'W' seldom end abruptly in six days – not without drastic measures. In the world she's from, history is something painted and plastered over. But surely dreams function differently from reality and, in all likelihood, this is just a simple chronicle.

This is how the Academy of Greatest Learning was founded. To this day, the Vermillion Gate glows whenever one of the founders – the Ice Dragon or I – passes through it. I find it a bit embarrassing but Xue Long seems to like it. In fact, he was the one who built it that way.

Red Dust

7

The first thing she did when she woke up, instead of reaching for her phone, was to retrieve the disc from her drawer. It remained dark even when she shook it. She remembered the question it posed.

Do you consent to enter into a parallel universe?

Was the dream world the 'parallel universe' the disc referred to? Her first night at the academy coincided with the day the mysterious package arrived. Did the disc really possess mystical powers to transport her into another world?

She turned over every inch of the disc and the cube. Nothing. No symbols, or markings of any kind on their scratchproof, reflective surfaces. It was like trying to guess at the thoughts of someone wearing mirrored sunglasses. You only see yourself, while the other person remains safely sequestered away.

The other explanations veered into the realm of past lives, reincarnation or simply confabulation. The last possibility was particularly disquieting because it would mean there was something wrong with her brain physiologically, or with her mental health. A quick search on the internet turned up nothing. Most of the information was published by laypeople and semi-professionals at most, dealing with a recurring scenario, not a continuous series like hers. She read that an average person has three to five dreams at night. Indeed, seven is not unheard of, but mostly dreamt and not remembered. She could vividly recall her sequential dreams.

For now, she decided there was no need to do anything about it. These dreams were hurting no one as far as she could tell. She slept, she dreamt, she went to work the next day. Even if she booked an appointment with a shrink or a neurologist, she did not know what to tell them. *I am having these dreams where I am a novice summoner at the Academy of Greatest Learning.* She might get herself admitted into an institution. Or laughed out of the park. Probably both.

The most important thing at hand was to get herself ready for the potluck that evening. Here was a chance for her to be reborn. No one expected her to remain the same as her teenage self. She watched interviews with celebrities, scanning the comments for moments which viewers found appealing, and practised the *eye smiles*, looking over her shoulder and putting her finger on her lips in front of the mirror. She recorded her voice and played it back to herself. Should she sound sweet, high-pitched and delightful, or low, smoky and sensual? She would be an amalgam of everything people found attractive.

She rehearsed until it was time for her appointment at the hair salon to get a blowout. She had chosen one that was on the way to the wine shop where she would pick up a *prestige cuvée* champagne. Most people would bring a casserole, finger food or a salad to a potluck. She thought champagne would be an impressive, sophisticated choice. She considered going for a manicure and a pedicure but the cost was climbing and hair would make more of an impression than nails.

The hair salon was all black leather and gleaming metal. She had selected a slightly pricier one in hopes it would translate to better service. She showed the celebrity photo to the stylist, also sleekly attired in black, whose nametag read 'Josephine'.

'I see, so you want your fringe to fall softly on both sides of your face, and your hair to be half up and the rest to cascade down in loose waves.'

The description sounded good, so she nodded, a flash of that curtain of silk from a distant world glimmering across her mind.

'Would you like the *Nano-HydroSpa Rejuvenating* hair treatment or the *Silk Therapy Bio Renewal-X* hair treatment?'

'What?'

'The *Silk Therapy Bio Renewal-X* treatment contains—' here Josephine rattled off a rhapsodic list of ingredients, '—whereas the *Nano-HydroSpa Rejuvenating* treatment contains—' another list, equally aureate, '—to help your hair recover its lost moisture. I recommend the *Nano-HydroSpa Rejuvenating* treatment. More expensive, but better.'

'I just want to get a blowout.'

'I understand, but to achieve the result in the photo, I highly recommend a hair treatment first.'

'That's fine, I'll just get the blowout without the hair treatment.'

'But your hair is so dry! It's the frizzy type and lacking in lustre. How about the *Silk Therapy Bio Renewal-X* then, if you're budget conscious?'

She bit her lip.

'Let me think about it,' she said, getting up to leave.

'No, no, sit, sit. No hair treatment? Okay, suit yourself.'

Josephine tugged on her hair a few times as she was styling it, she suspected on purpose. The curls were not as flowing and bouncy as she had hoped.

'It would have been better if you had got the hair treatment.'

On the train, she was browsing through Japanese *onsens* and was so close to paying for the first hot springs holiday of her life, before catching herself at the last minute. What was she doing? It was as if a strange guest had taken up residence inside her and was whispering suggestions that she was powerless to ignore. *You'll be able to see the moonlight amid the mountains like Thoreau.* But she had never liked travelling. *How do you know when you've never tried?* She did not have to try to know – the very thought of figuring out the bus schedule in Japanese to get to a remote mountain was already arduous. *EmpiMaps makes everything so easy. There's translation in EmpiMaps. Besides, you don't have to visit one in Japan. There are hot springs in other parts of the world that speak English. You can sleep in four-poster beds instead of futons. There'll be spas and breakfasts in bed. It'll be luxurious.* In the end, she bought a Zen table ornament with sand she could rake. She could already hear ianniechan in her head, chastising her for thinking she could possess an experience with something material.

The doorway was filled with shoes when she turned up at Estelle's apartment with the *prestige cuvée* in its black silk-ribboned holster. In her tote bag was an extra bottle of plum wine she got for herself.

Estelle greeted her by brushing their cheeks together – she had never seen Estelle do this with anyone when they were in school, which made her feel buoyant. This roomy flat outside the core district was rented, but Estelle actually owned a tenanted one-bedder in the core central region. About a third of their class were gathered in the living room, paper cups in hand. Some came with their spouses, but most came alone. Jerome was the only one who brought his kids as well, all three huddled with Estelle's two boys watching a programme on a tablet while the adults mingled. He and Estelle had kept in contact all these years. The rule of thumb was to be thirty minutes late but she was fifty, so she was the last to arrive. Everyone cooed over her entrance. Estelle gushed over the well-packaged gift when she handed it to her but did not remark upon what it contained. Perhaps she should have brought a curry of peacock tongues. No one complimented her hair.

The dining table had been moved to the living room. The salads were not harlequin-designed, nor were there pastry pigs and turkeys bewitched to a dark gold. Instead, all the usual suspects were present – fried noodles, chicken wings, potato salad. Most of the food had turned cold, having endured the air-conditioned car rides to the apartment and sitting out until the guests arrived. She felt an intense craving for a piping hot soup of snow fungus, apple and pork. They reminisced about their secondary school days. She heard stories she had never been privy to before – who was really in love with whom, the real culprits behind pranks. Perhaps the exact course of events had become muddied along the way. One of their classmates started watching *Love in the Snow* on her phone, unable to bear the suspense of being left hanging over the hero's fate any longer. *Sorry, I only meant to check out the first few minutes to see if Detective Kang survived* – which led to her checking out entirely.

'Ah, my wife's crazy about the show, too.'

Everyone ended up huddling around her phone. Estelle told her smart television to play the episode on the big screen. In the middle of the episode, Empi thanked viewers for their support and announced an extravaganza to celebrate their anniversary, which included a blitz of perks to reward both existing users and new sign-ups – special anniversary items for avatars, for instance, providing the same online shopping discount as her *Flower Rain* lashes. The benefit stacks for people like her, who already owned such items.

'You'd think with the stir #DeleteEmpi is creating, some regulations would begin to kick in somehow. But it seems Empi is coming back stronger than ever.'

'Haven't you heard? Ken Huang can't be indicted for anything. No matter what he does.'

'You mean the article that says he is the emperor of the world today? That he has something on everyone, so everything you can think of is under his influence – corporations, courts of law, even governments?'

'That's just gossip, no? I mean, how is that even possible?'

'The article pointed out several coincidences, though – key personnel who opposed Empi's development plans being mysteriously removed, either stepping down or capitulating. But most telling was the incident involving his son-in-law.'

'Oh.'

'Wasn't his son-in-law abducted after Arissa Huang killed herself, presumably because of her marital problems?'

'Official reports said it was depression, though.'

'The timing does seem a little fishy.'

'I heard the abductors had a grudge against him and he was hurt so badly he's still stuck in a medical facility in chronic pain.'

'And who do you think had the greatest grudge against him?'

'Ken Huang himself?'

'Exactly.'

According to the article, Arissa Huang first met her future husband, Li Yun Xi (李云熙) of Qing Yun Technology (青云科技), at the Artificial Intelligence World Conference. Empi and Qing Yun Technology were among the companies invited to speak, although Qing Yun was mired in rumours it was on the verge of bankruptcy.

The company's Yun Yun Chat (云云短信), YY for short, was developed to compete against Empi, containing many features not found in the latter, such as the ability to transcribe speech to text directly. Its clean, minimalistic interface was also welcomed by users who found the mammoth Empi becoming a bit unwieldy. It launched with a bang, to a whopping 5 million downloads within a month, a number that had taken Empi half a year to achieve. But the momentum did not last. In the end, Empi was too entrenched in their daily lives. Even though YY was the superior messenger, people were still using Empi for its other functions. Many users uninstalled the app when their friends did not jump on the bandwagon. Besides, it was such a shame to give up on their avatars, on their EmpiGrams, when they had been building them for years. In order to gain special abilities for their avatars, such as priority in queues, considerable time and effort had gone into levelling them – purchase by purchase, tap by tap.

The elder Huang had instinctively disliked his son-in-law. He was taken by surprise, actually, for the sallow Yun Xi was so unlike the baby-faced idols his daughter liked to date. The idols he did not mind, but something relentless about Li Yun Xi had reminded him of a climbing plant his mother had introduced into the garden when he was a boy, which overran the entire place with its rhizomes, seeds and runners.

All this was ostensibly told to the writer of the article by a friend of the family, who wished to remain anonymous.

'Wasn't there a much publicised falling-out just before they got married? Rumour has it that a large investment in Qing Yun Technology was actually Ken Huang paying Li to break up with his daughter.'

'Is it true that Li Yun Xi loved another woman, and he kept his lover close all this time? And that after four years of being unhappily married, Arissa Huang overdosed on antidepressants?'

'Well, they had been married for four years and yet there were no children.'

'Still, with a family background like that, she could have had any man she wanted. Why take it so hard?'

When they ran out of things to say, Estelle seized the opportunity to share how she had suffered from gout and the alkaline water machine she got helped to alleviate her condition. Jerome chimed in that he had also got the machine for his family and seen an overall improvement in general health. Both of them were now selling the machine, after experiencing its benefits. For the next hour, everyone was shown a demonstration of what the machine could do and offered a cup of alkaline water to drink. Two of their classmates said they had to return home. After another fifteen minutes, she too said she had to leave.

She was surprised to run into them at the void deck, blue smoke curling from their cigarettes.

'Did you see how she was sitting arching her back all night? I was about to ask her if she had a back problem!'

'And she kept flipping her hair, like, every minute? I was sitting behind her and after the third time I got smacked in the face, I made sure I was always at the other end of the room from her.'

Laughter.

Academy of Greatest Learning
8

A pearl-diver is seeking the fruits of the sandy birchleaf pear (沙棠) that prevents drowning.

Husband searching for a bird from Mount Xuan Yuan (轩辕山) to rid his wife of jealousy.

The chief of a murrain-plagued village has requested the red earth found in the river of the Brittle Mountains to apply on cattle.

In her breaks between classes, she often reads the bamboo supplications hanging outside the administration office, the names exotic and strange on her tongue. A grand building with a tall, sweeping roof like a 'resting mountain' (歇山顶), the administration office is located at the heart of the academy, serving as the nexus of communication with the outside world. Scribes receive requests for the services of summoners, transfer these on to bamboo plaques and string them in rows, where they make a clattering sound in the wind.

Since she entered the academy, life has fallen into the rhythm of gathering ingredients, crafting and summoning. She finds herself wanting to be able to go on these expeditions – indeed, learn all she can about this strange land, in the repose of that oneiric light filtering through the paper panels, the passage of time forgotten. One day she shall emerge, fully fledged, armed hopefully with one or two high-level elemental spirits, and spread her wings and fly to the furthest corners of this world, maybe adding one or two pages of her own to Chao Ying's manuscript: *300 li east of here is the Mountain XXX. Here you will find the Gibberishium Gobbledygookium whose cries are like turkey noise.*

That's going to take some time, says Brilliant Jade. You've to be a Junior Summoner at least to go on expeditions. No one's going to hire a novice. When you've gained enough experience, either from expeditions or summoning, you can request to be evaluated as a Summoner proper. I hear only ten per cent make it every year.

What do you have to do to be in the ten per cent?

You'll have to participate in major expeditions. Or summon a rare spirit. Last year, there was a senior who summoned a *Wen Yao* (文鳐). Displays of finesse like that are considered shoo-ins in the exam.

She looks up *Wen Yao* and discovers it is a winged cyprinid spirit that flies by night, 'whose cries are like a phoenix's'. Its sighting ensures a bumper harvest that year. Farmers must have rejoiced.

How can we be promoted to Junior Summoner, then?

The seniors say you'll have to pass some kind of Trial.

What Trial?

Brilliant Jade shrugs. They are very secretive about that.

She doesn't have to wait long to find out, for Master Cloud announces it that very day. The Novice Trial is the same every year – a rite of passage through Mount Ling Qiu (令丘山). Naturally, she is not expecting a stroll in the park – or mountain, in this case – but when Master Dawn takes them to a peak overlooking Mount Ling Qiu, she wonders at this vision of an elevated underworld. The mountain is devoid of any vegetation, and for a reason. As she watches, spiritous flames erupt on its slopes like solar flares. Baptism by fire, indeed.

The start and end points will be marked with flags, says Master Dawn. Your seniors and teachers will all be there to witness your – she winks – moment of triumph. Any questions?

How are we going to get through *that?* someone asks.

That's for you to find out, Master Dawn beams.

It becomes apparent the Trial is an all-round test of a novice's proficiency, from the knowledge of what to summon, and gathering the ingredients, to the actual crafting. Without the right elemental spirits, it is impossible to cross the mountain. What is needed is an elemental spirit with the ability to extinguish spirit fire. After poring through Chao Ying's tome, they narrow the possibilities to eight, all summoned with water stones, five of which are avian.

The three non-avian elemental spirits are the unicorn-like *Quan Shu* (臛疏), the ten-winged fish *Xi Xi* (鰼鰼) and the tortoise-like *Gui* (蛫). Like the *Wen Yao*, the *Quan Shu* and the *Xi Xi* are quasi-legendary. If any of the novices possess the ability to summon them, it is unlikely they will be taking the Novice Trial in the first place. As for the *Gui*, the ingredients that make up the summoning stone are located on a faraway mountain, so that option is ruled out as well.

Of the five birds, one is the legendary double-headed, four-legged *Lei* (鸓), while the owl-like *Qie Zhi* (窃脂) and the corvine *Zhi Tu* (駅駼) both have summoning stone ingredients that similarly must be gathered from distant mountains near the centre of the continent. That leaves only two possibilities: the Scarlet Pheasant (赤鷩) and the red-beaked, kingfisher-like *Min* (鴖).

They submit their findings to Master Cloud, who rewards them with a rare smile.

Little Hua Mountain (小华山) and Mount Fu Yu (符禺山) are mountains to the west where the ingredients for the summoning stones may be found. She is already thrilled to be visiting two strange mountains, even if they may be right outside the academy. Little Hua Mountain is supposed to be filled with wandering cattle and chime stones with high, clear timbres. But when she gets there with Brilliant Jade, they fail to find a single creeping fig needed for the Scarlet Pheasant. A few metres away, a wild cow munches on the grass.

The others must have come last night, says Brilliant Jade. Let's head over to Mount Fu Yu. Maybe we can find something there.

On the slopes of Mount Fu Yu, all they see are capering goats – they look and behave like normal goats, except for their beards, which are a deep and impossible red. Of the yellow fruits of the crimson sunflower, shaped like babies' tongues, for summoning their *Min*, there is no sign. The dozen or so sunflowers, almost her height, are completely bare. The few remaining are tightly closed.

Let's just collect something at least, she says. We can practise crafting a stone and come back sometime later. Perhaps there'll be new fruits then.

The resultant stew is darkly fetid, consisting of crushed crimson petals, hairs from a browsing red-bearded goat, scraped bark, scooped water from murky puddles, caked mud, suspicious scums, and a host of other nameless and curious matter that have caught their eyes.

Your crucible reflects your confused heart, says Master Zeno.

Trying to be experimental, she says.

Brilliant Jade chortles.

In contrast, Green Peak's section of the crucible is softly glowing with a blue light. He was part of the party of four who set off last night.

Well done, says Master Zeno, nodding.

She feels a stab of dismay in spite of herself. She *wants* to do well in the Trial.

It's all right, says Brilliant Jade. Maybe we can summon something even better with these. Who knows?

At least she has someone to comfort her. And she has made a joke somebody laughed at. Even if she has yet to accomplish anything.

紅
塵

Red Dust

9

There was a general effervescence in the air, like the last few minutes of class before the end of a school day. After two months, the holographic installation project was finally approaching its conclusion. The five interns selected by ZH, the project leader, were bent over more than usual at their temporary workspaces, hoping to make a good last impression. She forgot what ZH's real name was: presumably, it was hard to remember and hard to pronounce, so he said everyone could call him by his initials.

The area around her desk was usually an oasis of relative calm. People would meet her on the first day they arrived – she would probably be the one to show them to their interview room and then, if all went well, orientate them. After that, as long as their pay was credited into their bank accounts on the twenty-eighth of every month, there was little reason for them to approach her. She always processed paychecks on time.

Today however, two of the interns had approached her to ask if there were any entry-level job openings. But it was Jacq's visitation that surprised her.

'Hello,' said Jacq in a low voice so as not to startle her.

'Hi, Jacq.'

'We're wrapping up the project we've been working very hard on.'

'So I've heard, congrats.'

'*Hiryū no Yume*'s opening this Saturday. The team's gonna watch it together to celebrate. I remember you saying you're also interested in catching it. Would you like to join us? The interns are coming, too.'

A memory of laughter rose unbidden in her mind. This was no madeleine and lime-flower tea scented involuntary memory, but harsh and raucous. The scene at the void deck with its two characters, tendrils of smoke curling from their lips, rose up like a stage before her. She closed her eyes but the image, illuminated not by physical light, could not be blocked out that way.

'I'm sorry, but I've got something on that day.'

Jacq looked disbelieving for a moment, as though thinking what sort of plans she could possibly have.

Why should plans only exist in physical reality? As if people do not carry an invisible world within themselves. In many ways, the internal world is more persistent than external reality. A projector that keeps playing, ceaselessly, even in the dark. A recorder that cannot be silenced. Who is to say dreams are insubstantial when whole lives can be lived in their pursuit? Isn't everyone acting out their lives according to their dreams of themselves?

So what if her life seemed stalled because she would rather spend it with ghosts than in human sociality? As if she had boxed herself up and was prevented from moving forward. But what if no one is actually moving forward? Ghosts are perceived as stuck in limbo. But what if it's really everyone's lives that are spent in the waiting room? For the bus. For the train. For the work shift to be over. For the big break. To grow up. A character stuck in a mound of earth in a Beckett play – the visual representation of countless lives stuck in dead-end jobs, in marriages, in solitude. Humans project onto ghosts what they secretly fear about themselves.

To escape into dreams suggests running from reality, as if dreams are but its shadow. But what if dreams are removed from reality's shade and the reality of dreams recognised as different from the reality that governs matter?

A world not bound by the obduracy of matter becomes possible.

She was ready to pack up by six, but she waited for five minutes after six thirty before she actually made her move. Outside the office, the face of Park Min-jae, the current reigning superstar for his role as Detective Kang in *Love in the Snow*, smiled at her from video screens, billboards and store products, in part because he was the chosen ambassador for Empi's anniversary celebrations. Since she first heard the announcement at Estelle's, the company's trademark shade of luminous blue had begun to slather the walls of physical and online spaces. All were trapped like ants in molasses of blue. Blue light poured from LCD displays and stuck to the bodies around her, as sticky as tropical heat. The entire city was a screen; she an interface in the network. One day, after spending an hour and a half in a blue-wrapped train, her vision became shot through with fire. She made sure not to board blue trains after that. She bought the 14 Days Mask Pack that featured a different expression of the actor every single day, but skipped over the deep seawater mask on the tenth day. The box was blue.

Lives Ruined Watching Love in the Snow

Recently, the male lead of the hit drama has also taken the lead in the fantasies of many young women. The epidemic of 'Park Min-jae Lovesickness' is not as harmless as you might think, causing the Ministry of Security and Protection to post a warning on its official Empi channel against watching the popular drama.

What was newsworthy, as the article pointed out – she was reading the news as she waited for a train not blue to come along – was not the fact that many female members of the audience had fallen under the charms of the male lead, but that officials had deemed it significant enough to issue a warning in the name of public security. Screenshots of case studies explaining the 'very real' troubles viewers had got themselves into were attached to the post.

In California, a twenty-four-year-old husband was so jealous of his wife's admiration for Park Min-jae that he became obsessed with editing images of himself to create an Empi persona resembling the actor. In a photo of him walking the dog in a park taken by his wife, from a time they weren't estranged, his once sandy hair was an uncanny dark cloud. The highlights were strangely smoky, giving the hair the matte quality of a black rubber tyre. No matter how much he tried, he could not get the sun to shine on black hair.

> *Perhaps you may think there's nothing overtly wrong with Smith's actions, but the inordinate amount of time needed to transform into another persona may cause him to neglect his life and job. It may lead to absenteeism from work, or withdrawal from his friends and family at a time when he needs the most support.*

The case study even extrapolated his criminal conduct:

> *Smith may be driven to even more outrageous acts as a result of not being able to achieve the effect he wants, such as resorting to scams in order to procure the luxury threads found on the actor. He may be charged for violent or disorderly conduct while intoxicated, in an attempt to escape from his troubles.*

She continued to scroll through the other cases, such as a man in Italy paying a hefty sum for plastic surgery to look more like a *flower boy* in order to regain his wife's affection (which may tempt him to misappropriation of funds in order to pay for the surgery). The case studies, she realised, were not actually case studies but speculations of crimes not yet committed, interspersed with advice on the right approach to watching dramas. Oddly, every screenshot was emblazoned with the actor's pixieish face, so she felt like she was looking at his photo album instead. Elsewhere, it was noted that the brand of skincare he endorsed was sold out in stores. Also, the rice cooker, clothing, accessories, beverages, massage chair, coffee shop and car that appeared in the show were enjoying brisk sales. All these – and more! – could be found on EmpiBazaar, while stocks lasted.

She got off at the bayfront station, along with the rest of the carriage. Today was the day all the hype was leading up to – the anniversary of Empi's launch in this city all these years ago. The entire bay area, with its skyline of iconic architecture, would be flooded with blue, serving as a stage for a holographic light show. Several local artistes – apparently big names but she was not in tune with the local arts scene – would be performing theme songs from Empi's most popular content. Park Min-jae had been specially flown in yesterday and tickets to the fan meet had been snapped up within seconds. Since she had been unable to get a ticket, she decided to take a trip to the bay, hoping to catch a glimpse of the star crooning – or lip-syncing – the drama's soundtracks. In the end, she was not able to wedge herself into any of the buildings overlooking the concert but stood instead in the middle of a park, watching the telecast on her phone with other spectators, under an animated sky illuminated with dancing mirages, like messages written in the heavens by a god. Bright, brilliant blue is the colour of divinity across many religions. No one questions a devotee falling in love with a deity through a sacred text, the texture of their relationship spelled out by the warp and weft of words, but devotion for a persona out of a spun tale is immediately suspect. What is true in both cases is that demented acts have been committed in the name of such love.

*

When she stepped out of her building's lift, she was chagrined by the hillock of parcels flooding the recess area in front of her apartment. The gate of her neighbour's unit was shut but the door stood open, even though it was past midnight. When the old lady heard the sound of the lift, she came to the doorway with her watering can.

'I'm so sorry,' she said, stacking up the boxes and clearing a path for the woman. 'I told them many times to place the boxes neatly, but they just don't listen.'

'So many things to buy nowadays,' her neighbour remarked.

Her quick disappearance into her apartment was hindered by the mountain of parcels spilling out of the entrance. The old lady tried peering across but she shut the door, cutting off her view.

Parcels lined the apartment from floor to ceiling. She had not found time to assemble the canopied bed. It had taken a while to find a bronze mirrored dressing stand. It might be a kitschy imitation, but the ones in antique shops were way beyond what she could afford. The low square table with the slender feet was a near-perfect replica of the one in her room at the academy. Other objects like the crimson sunflowers, lacquerware – designs painstakingly drawn with the underarm hair of rats – teaware, candlestand, incense implements and indoor waterfall were unpacked but unarranged. The literati dreamt of a reclusive, contemplative life but, she noted wryly, the assembly of objects around her appeared to belong more to a modern-day *hikikomori* rather than the scholar-recluse. No matter. They were totems, talismans, assemblages against mundanity.

On the windowsill, the sunflowers bent towards the night.

太
学

Academy of Greatest Learning

10

The water stones turn out to be grumous lumps, hardly solid at all. Even Brilliant Jade loses confidence they may be pleasantly surprised by them.

I can already see the worms' soft bodies coming out of these, groans Brilliant Jade.

Green Peak's stone, on the other hand, scintillates with blue fire. Master Zeno regards it with approval.

Don't be dazzled just by the appearance of his stone, says Master Zeno. What's inside is the most important. The structure, whether it is in disarray. Size and sparkle are merely superficial.

Privately, she thinks stones that are beautifully arranged inside almost always reflect this on the outside. No one is surprised when Green Peak summons his Scarlet Pheasant. They do not try to summon anything, because of Brilliant Jade's paranoia that a worm will tumble out of the portal – not that she herself is particularly keen for that to happen. Brilliant Jade manages to obtain some of his withered leftover vines. His generosity, along with the fact that he released his menagerie of worms after summoning the Scarlet Pheasant, makes Brilliant Jade less furious with him.

The flames in the crucible exercise a hypnotic fascination over her. She sees whole universes bloom and collapse in on themselves. Flame gazing, she knows, is a common meditation technique. According to Master Zeno, when a summoner gazes upon the crucible, all they are looking at is themselves. She watches as a tendril of fire leaps up and takes the shape of a bird accompanying a traveller through a fiery mountain path, or the disciples on the road to Emmaus, or Krishna and Arjuna, or Moses and Al-Khiḍr – refrains of the chorus of the 'magical travelling companion' Jung discusses in a book relating psychology to alchemy. The comrade who goes through life at one's side. The solitary ego who finds a mate in itself.

Another flare illuminates the crucible. She doesn't want *just* another Scarlet Pheasant, but an ally she can call her own. She recalls all the strange ingredients, organic and inorganic, in the recipes found in Chao Ying's book and throws in a lock of her hair. Hair, *qing si* (青丝), meaning 'green threads'. She loves this expression, for its depth, its secret hint of green lingering in the black, and also the webby entanglement of thread-like hair, hair-like threads, winding their way around the heart, coiling, twining, aching, until one is winded and breathless. Ties that link as well as enchain. Add the radical for 'heart' to make the almost homophonous *qing* (情), spoken in a rising tone. *Qing si* (情丝) – amorous threads.

She isn't thinking of that kind of love when she tosses in her lock of hair, especially considering the veritable armada of worms summoned by her classmates. Not exactly. She isn't that far gone yet. But when she thinks about it, the entire process of summoning – from knowing the combination of the ingredients to the contract making, seems to be imbued with a kind of intimacy. She wouldn't spill her secrets to just anybody, and she wouldn't bind herself to another human being so readily either. She considers throwing in her blood, but that has somehow become too obvious, too common. A lock of hair feels more elegant.

As the hair disintegrates, and its constituent carbon, hydrogen, nitrogen and whatever atoms it is made up of insert themselves into the stone forming in the igneous depths of the crucible, she makes a wish for the stone to bring her an elemental spirit who will become another familiar friend.

The stone she retrieves from the crucible is translucent, like a raw diamond – which she recalls is a crystal structure of carbon. About the size of a snowflake, its interior is streaked with flecks of white, like flying snow. It is not a particularly pretty stone and she is slightly disappointed, both by its size and nondescript appearance. Nonetheless, it is a stone of sound structure and she sews a pocket on the inside of her student robes, right next to her heart, to bring it to the next summoning class. Holding it against the candlelight and gazing into the snowy maelstrom, she wonders what it will bring.

With everyone getting better at crafting, more of their classmates' stones are able to ensnare worms, much to Brilliant Jade's distress. A hail of worms later, two more students manage to snag a Scarlet Pheasant and a *Min*, to envious applause, making it a total of three people who have managed to summon the required elemental spirits for the Trial, all from Green Peak's party.

Anyone else wants to try today? Master Dawn asks.

She looks at Brilliant Jade, who shakes her head. In spite of the ingredients from Green Peak, Brilliant Jade was unable to craft anything more solid.

Once she is sure that no one else is going to respond, she steps forward.

Master Dawn acknowledges her with a nod.

Reaching inside the collar of her robes, she brings out the water stone warmed by her heart's blood and pitches it upwards. Suspended briefly in the air, it catches the weak rays of the morning sun filtering through layers of the mountain mists and shines for a moment like a second sun. Everyone's eyes are trained on the stone. It remains in the air for a heartbeat, two. It seems like a gateway will not open. Then it happens – just as the stone appears to be about to fall and scatter into dust.

A portal opens. Blinding white.

She has to shield her eyes.

What is it?

She hopes it is not a giant white worm.

A man descends from the sky, his white robes swirling around him like snowdrifts, his ebony-black hair reaching to his waist, lifting in the breeze. Everyone's attention is held by this apparition, whose lips are crimson as though painted and whose eyebrows are black as if darkened with kohl. She has long noticed the picturesqueness of this world but in this being, surely it has reached its apotheosis. Although everyone looks like they could be on the runway or in showbiz, they are mere mortals compared to this otherworldliness.

There are bloody gashes on his face that look quite deep. Dimly, she worries they will leave a scar on his skin, which has the translucence of jade, and her heart twinges strangely at the thought. His complexion is like peach blossoms in the faint warmth of spring. To have the fortune of peach blossoms, it is said, is to be entangled in love. She has no doubt that, with such a face, he will have many entanglements.

Has he been engaged in some sort of tussle? Now that he is standing on level ground, and the light has faded and the wind has died down, his robes are not as pristine as they first appeared. Indeed, in some places, the cloth has been shredded into ribbons.

They stare at each other like this for a while, Master Dawn and her classmates looking on, until he clicks his tongue impatiently, shaking her out of her daze.

W-welcome, she stutters, then cringes at herself. *Welcome what?*

The elemental spirit looks at her coldly.

She clears her throat.

Are you, um… a worm? At these words, his kohl-black eyebrows shoot up until they disappear under the hair falling across his forehead. One that has attained a higher level of cultivation? she hurriedly continues. His eyebrows do not unknit. Maybe? she squeaks.

The pale morning, not very warm to begin with, becomes decidedly chilly. She looks at the blood on his face, his torn robes, and suddenly feels fear in the pit of her stomach.

Who in the world is this?

She turns to Master Dawn for help.

Master Dawn mouths the word, Contract.

W-would you like to form a contract with me? she asks. No, she corrects herself, I want to form a contract with you.

The elemental spirit stares at her for a few seconds. Then suddenly, his mirthful laughter rings out across the summoning field, deep and resonant.

See if you can, he smiles, a portal opening behind him.

He turns, but at the last moment looks back. Casually, as though they were talking about the weather, he says, I'm not a worm. I'm a *dragon*. The Ice Dragon, in fact. The founder of your academy.

With a final smirk, he disappears through the portal.

Red Dust

II

She was in such a state of distraction that she made several errors in the update of sales orders, which she had to correct. How could that be the Ice Dragon?

It was just too implausible.

The pink of Post-its seen through the white of copier paper reminded her of the peach blossom complexion of a certain face. She shook her head vigorously to clear it. Inked writing on bamboo haunted the uniform typeface on her screen. In the cool fluorescent lights meant to foster productivity, she felt the muted presence of daylight from another world. It was probably imprudent, but she left ten minutes before six thirty.

Light was draining out of the sky when she emerged, wisps of clouds losing their definition and looking like lost souls suspended in the atmosphere. Once again, the daylight hours of her life had been guzzled by Verge Inc. and expelled as phlegmy darkness. She felt like Wang Zhi and all his variations, who stopped to watch two old men playing a board game, or four youths singing, or singing *and* playing a board game, only to find his implement – sometimes a riding crop, sometimes an axe handle – rotted, his horse turned to bones, his family deceased.

The measure of her days was in keyboard taps, the light she lived under electric. Among office workers, there was a high prevalence of vitamin D deficiency, in spite of the abundance of sunshine. Apparently, life behind glass and cosmetics filtered out the essential rays.

Even the artists. Was this the aesthetic life they wanted, or did it turn out to be anaesthetic? She knew Alex had come close to quitting several times but could not because his wife was expecting their first child. There was a short film he had been working on for several years: he'd wanted to enter it into a competition but could not make the deadline. She had seen an earlier clip he sent to the group chat for feedback, something of an animated fever dream of a battle between ant-like creatures and fungal invaders, obviously zombie-ant fungus inspired. To survive, the eusocial insects agreed to surrender their consciousness, as long as the sun was in the sky for the benefit of the fungus, commuting to towers with the right conditions for the fungus to thrive. She thought the imagery was intricate – baroque, a ballet of pseudopodal shapes – for the first thirty seconds. The latter three-quarters looked noticeably less detailed. The winner last year was his art school junior – single, living with his parents. Although Alex had added his congratulations to the never-ending string under the post, he had been visibly shaken, watching the award-winning film on loop. The jejune had grown, while he was still scrabbling in the dust. Once, he had been the recipient of such congratulations, as valedictorian, landing the job at Verge. Once.

She travelled home surrounded by people living double lives. The train doors opened and a time traveller squeezed in, shoving her backwards into a rancher who did not look up from feeding glowing hay to a unicorn, pelt shining like quicksilver. Floating above the creature's head, near the tip of its spiralling horn, was a steadily filling heart meter. All around her, people were absorbed in fabulous content, whether it was watching Josie Wong as a fox spirit, or battling, catching, raising – kirins, dragons, chimeras, unicorns, manticores. A parallel fantastic universe.

She was pleased to find her bulk order of sleeping pills on her doorstep – she had bought a variety to prevent drug tolerance. Expedited delivery had been worth it. The whine of the drill had hit her the moment she stepped off the bus. It was time again for electrical rewiring, one of those 'cyclical works' carried out on a regular basis for maintenance – something she looked forward to as much as menstruation. 'The same QUALITY, CONVENIENCE and COMFORT, regardless of the age of your block!' declared multiple digital display panels all over the estate. In the past, she took note of the 'EXPECTED DATE OF COMPLETION', holding it close like some eschatological date when she would be delivered from her auditory hell, until she observed the eternal recurrences of such projects. There were always upgrades to be done – to circuitry, to pipes, to pumps; cables re-laid, buildings re-roofed, linkways re-constructed. While she was at work, a fence had been built over the footpath and now she had to take a detour to get to the economy rice stall.

Clambering over boxes to get to her kitchen, she made a cup of chamomile tea to take with her pills. She had reduced her nightly routine to just removing her make-up, doing away with dinner and leaving her shower to the following morning. The blasts of the drill felt like physical blows but when she peered out of the window, there was no visible construction site – just endless rows of flats obscuring her view. Once again, her assailant was omnifarious and unknown. It might not be electrical rewiring, or even within the estate but on a bordering road – in which case jurisdiction would lie with some other department. Guidelines accompanied by cute cartoons on the website stated drilling and hammering should be avoided between ten thirty at night and seven in the morning. She checked her phone – it was only nine. She stuffed her ears with foam and switched on her bedside lamp, newly bought, which functioned as a sleep aid by emitting a soft, rhythmically pulsing light.

She tossed and turned, reaching for the place on the other side, where the mundanity of the world would stop, melatonin-induced black at the end of a film.

Make no mistake, mundaneness – it can grind a person down. Note the unmistakeable tang of soil in the word 'mundane', from *mondain* – 'of this world, worldly, earthly, secular' in Old French. In Chinese, life in this world is literally written as 'red dust' – referring to the earth kicked up in the air by ceaseless traffic. So everyone wanders in this mortal realm, stirring up dust, until they become dust themselves.

Academy of Greatest Learning

12

She is waylaid everywhere she goes – in the dining hall, in between classes along the corridors. Nobody can talk about anything else but what took place at the summoning field.

There is no respite, even during classes.

In the middle of the evening lecture with Master Cloud, a student raises his hand, causing her to pause in mid-sentence.

You over there, she says.

Master Xiao Yun, with all due respect, rather than talk about theories, shouldn't we ask the person who has actually summoned the White Dragon?

A deathly hush falls upon the classroom. Nobody breathes as they wait to see how Master Cloud will respond. Brilliant Jade bristles.

Hey, haven't you had enough? Brilliant Jade says. Give us all a break, will you?

Nobody here wants a break, he counters, looking around the classroom.

Heads bob in agreement.

Master Cloud's face twitches. There is the decorum of the class to be upheld but she is first and foremost a scholar on the bible for summoners. Her curiosity wins out.

You, Master Cloud says, turning to her. How would you increase the efficacy of the web cast by a summoning stone?

Here we go again.

I didn't do anything special, she says for the umpteenth time. I threw the stone into the air, just like everybody else. You can verify this with Master Xiao Chen.

What was the angle of the throw? someone asks.

What time was it? Was it early in the morning? Or late? another voice pipes up.

Master Cloud raises a hand to quiet the rising tumult.

I just tossed the stone upwards, she answers. As for the time, our summoning class was after breakfast. He said he was a dragon, but there's no proof other than his words. Didn't Grandmaster Chao Ying say it's impossible to summon one of the Dragon Gods?

At this, the commotion rises again.

But he can open dimensional portals!

My friend who was in that class said the elemental spirit made icicles rain from the sky!

Who said that? She wants to sock that person. Sure, there had been a sudden chill, but it could have been just a gust of cold wind.

There were definitely no icicles, she emphasises. Right, Ming Yu?

Right, Brilliant Jade confirms.

What were the ingredients for the stone? This question comes from Master Cloud herself.

Again, there wasn't anything special, she says. I put in my own hair, if you must know. After the incident, I gave some of my hair to Master Zeno. He tried crafting something from it and a perfectly ordinary stone resulted. There's nothing special about my hair at all.

Silence descends upon the class once more. This time, there is something calculating about the silence that gives her the chills.

Someone is waiting for her by the pebbled pathway when she returns to her room that evening. He is standing in the shadows, so she does not see him at first. When she comes close, he steps out into the light of the stone lantern, startling her. She recognises him as the one who interrupted Master Cloud's lecture before.

Sorry to have scared you, he grins.

The stone lantern lights him from below, making it look like he has stepped out from a movie of the horror genre. She looks over his shoulder – the lights in Brilliant Jade's room are out. There will be no help from there.

What's up? she says, pushing past him.

I just want to thank you for answering all our questions so readily today, he says, trailing after her. Your responses have been really helpful.

Don't worry about it. It's nothing.

She halts outside her door.

Let me do something for you.

Really, you don't have to.

Why don't I clean up your room a little for you? he insists, removing a brush and dustpan from a cloth bag she only notices now that he is carrying.

Can this guy be any more transparent? No way is she letting him into her room. She runs her fingers through her hair and a few strands come loose. She hands them over to him.

Just take these and leave.

He can hardly contain his excitement as he takes them from her.

Many thanks, he says. But he makes no move to go.

What now?

Do you think it may be possible… he begins in a show of hesitation. Would you be so kind as to give… a few more, please? Just in case, he adds.

What nerve!

She combs her hair once more with her fingers and gives him the dislodged strands.

Many thanks, he repeats. See you again.

I'd rather not see you here again, if possible.

Yes, yes. Of course, he says, retreating backwards down the path. He does not seem unduly perturbed. She wonders if he will heed her words.

She usually enjoys learning more about this world but, owing to the ridiculousness of the situations she has been subjected to, she decides to skip class the next day and hide out at Master Dawn's, who lives outside the school grounds in a log cabin at the edge of the forest. Passing through the Vermillion Gate early in the morning to avoid being seen, she picks her way down the mountain path.

The morning mist cloaks everything in a fragile softness, contributing the surreality she feels, if it's even possible to make a dream world even more surreal than it already is. Nothing seems fully solid, surely not the trees woven out of shadow, nor the glaucous cliffs in the distance. Outside of the academy, the tension leaves her muscles and she lets out a long breath. No matter how she looks at it, it is unimaginable she has summoned this elemental spirit. His human form alone points to a high level of cultivation. Most likely, her summoning stone had disintegrated and the portal opened simply because he happened to be passing by.

Master Dawn's cabin comes into view. The master is out front, pulling out weeds in her garden. She looks up when she hears her approaching footsteps and smiles.

Why, if it isn't our famous dragon summoner!

She responds by making a face. Not you, too!

Master Dawn laughs.

She explains her predicament to Master Dawn, who listens with a sympathetic expression she remembers from all those years ago.

You haven't had breakfast yet, have you? Master Dawn says.

She shakes her head.

Come on in, then. I have some porridge cooking. We can have it together.

Breakfast is a warm and comforting soy milk-based porridge made with lily bulbs and Chinese yam. She knows this porridge. She loves it. She makes special trips to the restaurant specialising in Nanjing cuisine just to have it. *Mei Ling* porridge, named after Madame Chiang Kai-shek. The story goes that when Madame Chiang *gave no thought for her rice and tea*, the chef whipped this up in a bid to reinvigorate her appetite. It worked, and the dish became a favourite of hers.

She is the dreamer, so it isn't surprising Master Dawn knows this dish, but she feels a certain discomfiture all the same, when this world shows signs of solipsism such as this.

After breakfast, Master Dawn makes tea. They sit around the table, holding their cups, the fragrance of mountain oolong filling the kitchen.

That day, do you think it was really the White Dragon? she asks Master Dawn.

Who knows, Master Dawn shrugs. Whoever he is, he's a spirit who can traverse dimensions, and there aren't many of them, really. Good job! she beams.

It has nothing to do with me and you know it, she says, exasperated.

I wouldn't be so sure, Master Dawn says. Why don't you consider the possibility there may be something special hidden in you, waiting to get out?

In spite of herself, she blushes with pleasure. How many years of her life has she spent wishing that were true? Perhaps in this world, her wish can be fulfilled.

She spends the day helping out around the cabin – tending to the vegetable garden and taking care of Master Dawn's elemental spirit, a *You Yan* (幽鴳), which looks like a striped macaque. She likes to laugh, so Master Dawn named her Xi Xi (嬉嬉), which means 'laughter'. Whenever there are visitors, she will fall to the ground and pretend to sleep.

Master Dawn is very well travelled. Her own aspirations of exploring the land are due in part to the time she spent having tea here in this cabin, during which Master Dawn shared stories about the things she has seen. Master Dawn did everything the long way, not having a dimension-traversing elemental spirit, which is what really impresses her. Elemental spirits who can traverse dimensions usually have also attained human form, which makes the master–servant dynamics uncomfortable for her. The War is over and so there is no more need for contracts to be made, in her opinion. In fact, Xi Xi is not summoned, but an elemental spirit that Master Dawn met on one of her travels.

These are strange views for a summoning teacher to have, she remarks.

Is that so? Master Dawn says. I have nothing against summoning. It may well have saved us from annihilation. Who knows when we may need it again, in the future?

If she thinks by absenting herself from the academy she can give her followers the slip, she is mistaken. There is a crowd outside her quarters when she gets back, disturbing the tranquillity of the rock garden she shares with Brilliant Jade. Quite a few bear packages that look like gifts. Have they come all the way here because they think she is convalescing at home? She shudders at the thought.

Brilliant Jade is standing on her verandah, watching the scene and glowering at all of them. When she catches sight of her returning in the distance, her eyes widen. Checking to see no one is looking, Brilliant Jade makes a covert shooing motion with her hand. She takes the hint and turns around.

The cold moonlight bathes the Vermillion Gate in a preternatural glow so it almost looks like an entryway to another world. She can think of nowhere else to go except back to the cabin and ask if Master Dawn will put her up for the night – or nights, until her problem can be solved. Pale hibiscus flowers, ghostly in the moonlight, sway in the night breeze and put forth their dusky scent.

Not for the first time, she is mesmerised by this world of mist and shadows, where the light is somehow always nocturnal, characterised by a certain indifference to morning, no matter how bright. So she is completely taken by surprise when a rough sack is pulled over her head, plunging her in darkness and filling her nostrils with a mouldy reek. Her arms are pinioned behind her back, her legs are knocked out from under her, and her wrists and ankles restrained by ropes. She fights to keep her balance as she is dragged off the main path. She tries to scream, only to have her assailant jerk on the drawstring of the sack, choking her off. He must have brought his face close to her, for she can feel the moistness of his breath through the material of the sack.

Cooperate with us – we don't want to hurt you, he says in a low voice.

Us. There is more than one of them. She can only hope the speaker will make good on his word.

She is supported under the arms by one person on each side. From the growing stillness of the air, she guesses they are leaving open ground and heading deeper into the cover of trees. She is shoved against a tree trunk. Her kidnappers remove the sack from her head, but keep her face pinned against the trunk of the tree so she can neither see their faces, nor tell how many of them there are. The coarse bark scrapes her cheek.

What do you want from me? Fear constricts her throat so her voice is barely a whisper.

They do not answer immediately and she thinks for a moment that they did not hear her, but then one of them speaks up.

Something that won't hurt you very much to give. Your hair.

She wants to weep.

The iron grip on the back of her head does not slacken but the hands gathering her hair into a bunch at the base of her neck are moist and clammy, betraying the nervousness of her would-be hairdresser. It seems her assailants are not equally sure of themselves. It probably makes no difference, but still, she feels slightly better. She feels a sawing motion, but before the strands can be harvested, the air shimmers in a way she has come to associate with the opening of a dimensional portal.

With her head fixed in place, she cannot see but rather senses the shock of her abductors. The sawing stops and the pressure holding her shifts just a fraction. She takes advantage of their momentary lapse in attention by slamming her body back with all her might. Instinctively, they leap aside to avoid her and she crashes to the ground. Now, she can take a good look at her captors.

There are four of them, none of whom she recognises. Seniors then? They glance back and forth from her to the man who has just materialised out of thin air.

It is the white-robed elemental spirit from the other day. She understands her attackers' astonishment because his unearthly appearance is like an assault to one's senses. She remembers the twinge she felt in her heart when she first laid eyes on him. To look at him is to forever be thirsty, like being doomed to chase after a miraculous dream.

The elemental spirit seems just as surprised to be there. He looks worse than he did previously. The cuts on his face have healed, but there are fresh bruises in their place. His clothes are stained the distinct pink of blood.

How long has this guy been here? one of her attackers hisses. Now they've both seen our faces!

The boy holding the razor, most likely the one with the moist, clammy hands, is shaking now. Eyeing him with contempt, the one who spoke snatches the razor from him and points it at the intruder. The elemental spirit, however, holds up a hand.

Please, continue. I did not intend to travel here. For some reason, I've been coming here often lately.

He's just going to leave? She gazes at him in disbelief.

Long moments pass, but he does not move. He remains where he is, frowning.

Well? the senior with the razor says. Scram already!

The elemental spirit turns contemplative. I would like to, he says, but it seems for some reason, I can't. He looks at her. I suspect it has something to do with her.

He sighs. This business is trickier than I thought.

Razor Boy yelps and the blade falls, skittering across the ground. He clutches his frostbitten hand, which has turned a vivid shade of purple.

You should get that treated quickly, says the elemental spirit. You could lose that hand.

Blubbering, Razor Boy stumbles back. His companions follow suit, similarly inarticulate noises issuing from their throats. They scramble over each other to get away.

There are just the two of them left.

She knows she should be just as frightened of this inhuman entity, who can possibly maim with just a glance, but she cannot hold back a sarcastic remark.

That was amazingly righteous, just now.

The elemental spirit does not look away.

Let's conclude this unfinished business. The summoning bond between us, it shall be no more after tonight. I've no intention of making a contract with you.

The air in front of him wavers once more, and a dimensional portal opens.

Wait! she cries out.

He stops, to her surprise.

Untie me before you go, at least, she pleads.

Sighing, he kneels before her, white light congealing in his right hand. A shard of ice appears, sharp as glass. He slices through the bonds binding her wrists and ankles. As he steps back into the shimmering light of the portal, however, a star flies from nowhere, burying itself deep into his shoulder. He inhales sharply, a fresh patch of red blossoming. She winces. *That must hurt.*

Where do you think you're going? a disembodied voice says, almost playfully.

Red Dust

13

Time dripped with the viscosity of pitch.

Jacq's latest photoshoot on EmpiGram had gone somewhat viral, approaching 10,000 likes – usually it's in the hundreds.

'Do you think it's because of the clothes? Or the background?' Jacq asked no one in particular.

'Both, maybe?' Nick said.

A patch of forest had surfaced in Empi consciousness recently. Slated for residential development, conservationists had propagated videos of its lost, fairy-tale beauty with its alien-looking trees, still, muddy pools and haunting cries of raptors piercing the silence. She had no doubt the trending hashtag had propelled Jacq's photos to their momentary stardom. It was also pretty ironic that this secondary forest, which bulbuls and turtles with labels like 'vulnerable' and 'critically endangered' called home, had been flattened to a photographic backdrop.

'I had to discard the dress because it was all torn and muddy, but it was worth it, I guess.'

'Of course! They may even re-zone the forest due to the public attention,' Alex said.

I don't think so, she said, mentally conversing with her colleagues, as she was wont to do. *Only the most significant tracts of rainforest are gazetted as nature parks. Though lamentable, the bulbuls and turtles will just have to keep to these areas –*

no more, no less. Public attention is double-edged. Already the incessant pounding of feet has made its way into the forest, crushing delicate shoots and leaflets. Some orchids thought to be locally extinct have been all but beaten into the dust.

The forest would be digitalised, just like everything else: another place where visitors may traipse through on its website, the electronic afterlife where things go after they vanish – ice, organisms, landmarks, cultures, modes of existence – the epitaph called history over its tombstone.

Finally, she feigned illness and texted Jayson to get the rest of the day off, leaving the office to variations of 'Get well soon'. If they suspected her ruse because it was Friday, they gave no sign of it. When she got home, however, it became clear she would not be finding out the owner of the voice soon. It felt like the drill was boring into her own skull. Wandering through her house, she ascertained that the noise was lowest in the living room and excavated a space to move her mattress to. Still, she wished for a dose of commiseration with her antihistamines, so she logged into Empi. Users in the same situation were already there.

shelterfanatic: I know I should be thankful for all these amenities being built but I'm just so very tired from all this construction ALL the time. Do we really need ALL these sheltered walkways?
Hiryuuuuu: I'd rather use my umbrella.
P4TR1CK527: Go back to your school/office or the library to work.
parkminjaeluv: Library is filled with folks blasting EmpiStream.
tgif168168: That's not the point. House should be a place for rest.
echoesinthevoid: I miss the days when they used brooms instead of leaf blowers.

P4TR1CK527: Do you have a better solution?
tgif168168: Petition for flats with noise insulation. Legislate for funerals and weddings to be conducted in function halls instead of void decks. There are companies that produce quieter leaf blowers. Surely we can afford that. We just have not made noise reduction a priority.
helpme9499: Too noisy to even start a petition.

When workers arrived with chainsaws to trim the branches off the trees, she relocated her mattress to the kitchen. She could scarcely lift a finger under the onslaught, only retreat as her house was taken over. EmpiStream was barely a strong enough opiate. In the middle of a video, she was shown a threatened species of ibex, as if someone had reached in and pulled out an image of the red-bearded goat on Mount Fu Yu from her mind. A sunny blur had given the animal a bushy beard of light, lens flare red. If she closed her eyes, she could picture the filaments of incarnadine she had spent almost a whole afternoon collecting from the tips of needles and leaves with Brilliant Jade.

She fled to the zoological park, which gave the impression of being in the middle of a lush tropical rainforest. It being a weekday, the toddler-toting half of the park's visitors were chasing dreams in glass and metal towers, and only the tourist half were ambling about, making it a perfect time for leaf-blowing. In this rainforest, leaf litter was not allowed to accumulate, but instead was transformed into dust tornados. She kept out of the way by trailing in the operator's wake, towards the ibex enclosure. The machine's ability to generate wind speeds of up to the highest devastation rating on all the disaster scales had inspired numerous videos of backyard hovercrafts. Human creativity in lifting clouds of dust into the air appeared to be boundless.

Compared to their EmpiStream counterparts scaling vertical cliffs, the ibexes in front of her, roving among cement rock piles, looked like robots. In fact, she wondered if they could not be replaced by animatronics – then there would not be the smell of sun-warmed ordure, and they need not be wrenched from their habitat, at least whatever was left of it. The same went for artefacts. If people were not so enamoured with what was real, then there would be fewer fiascos involving the return of stolen frescos. If only replicas were not discriminated against, we'd need not content ourselves with the poverty of reality. Humans would be able to transcend time. Bleached statues could regain their lost colour. Broken gods their lost limbs.

She stayed until the zoo's closing time. Even then, she still had four and a half hours before her exile was scheduled to end. The commute back would take an hour or so. She found a bench at the nearby park where she could sit with her phone.

She had fallen behind *Love in the Snow*, so preoccupied was she with the Novice Trial. She had almost forgotten how gorgeous the snowy landscapes in the show were. More than a mere setting for Park to romance his digital female lead, the snow had become almost a third, intangible interlocutor, whether frozen or falling, flurried or furrowed, slumbering unsunned on sills or faintly flickering against the streetlight. The camera would freeze upon a particular image, imbuing the scene with monumentality – the actors like characters on a frieze.

Even as a child, the digital world had provided comfort. Whenever she cried or made noise, her mother or nanny would push the phone into her hands. It was always warm, heated by the electrical impulses coursing through its innards. Encased in silicon, the stuff of breast implants and computer chips, it always felt like skin.

Dinner was a sandwich from a kiosk – a colloidal suspension of tuna particles in mayonnaise. She remembered the sandwich Alex's wife had made him one afternoon, chock-full of fish. Since then, it was an image for her of happiness.

太
学

Academy of Greatest Learning

14

An army of elemental spirits emerges from the shadow of the trees, human-faced and animal-limbed. She guesses there are about fifty of them. The one who spoke wears a live green snake coiling around each pricked ear. Judging from her commanding aura, she seems to be their leader. Her swaying steps are like those of a river goddess, making the gold threads on her robes flash. Her classically shaped face is exquisitely painted, highlighting her brows, like water ripples, her gloating safflower red lips.

Are they the pursuers whom the white-robed – now pink – elemental spirit has been trying to evade?

She steals a glance at the elemental spirit and feels a stab of pity. All his haughtiness has been drained out of him. With his pale face and blush robes standing out against the darkness, he reminds her of a lotus flower emerging from the silty depths of a pool, only to fade soon after.

How long has he been hounded like this? Is it her imagination, or did he just sway a little unsteadily on his feet?

He plucks out the star from his shoulder, examining its blackened tips.

Poison? he says softly.

Yes, Jade Frog Poison, the snake-adorned leader says with a smile. I'm surprised you're still standing.

The pink-robed elemental spirit turns to her, reproach in his gaze. Just so you know, this is all your fault. If it weren't for you… He trails off.

Me? What has this got to do with me? she argues. You offended them yourself.

In spite of her words, she feels guilt washing over her. If he had not stopped to help her, they probably would not have caught up with him.

Probably.

The army of elemental spirits begin to transform, losing their human features and falling onto all fours. Their clothes disappear under black fur as they take on increasingly caniform appearances – muzzles elongating, teeth and claws glinting in the moonlight. The air fills with an electrifying tension. There is no mistaking the heavy breathing, the madness in their eyes. They are going to rip him apart.

Stop! No! she cries out, before she realises what she is doing.

The hound nearest to her, whose form had been the female leader of the pack, turns slightly towards her. She could swear she is smiling, if it is possible to smile with a snout. The snakes at her ears bare their fangs, hissing, their sound like a live wire worming under her skin.

The hound readies herself to leap. Fifty sets of claws will sink themselves into his flesh. She will see the life leaving his body. In footages of disasters, nothing had cemented death for her more than the simple act of walking, of crossing over a threshold – the survivors stepping over motionless bodies when leaving the scene. Already the dead are becoming a piece of furniture, the life that used to be inside having moved on. The thought of his body becoming lifeless, like a piece of wood, fills her with an inexplicable sorrow. She does not want to witness it. She will try her hardest to prevent it, to preserve the glimmer of his existence upon this land.

She grabs the icy dagger lying on the grass and throws herself in front of him, swinging the weapon in a wide arc.

Swerving at the last moment, the hound narrowly avoids her throat being cut. A thin red line appears along her neck, oozing blood. She looks surprised, if the wide eyes on her canine face can be taken as surprise.

The pink-robed elemental spirit gazes at her in shock.

What are you doing? he says.

Can you open that portal again? I'll try to buy you some time. She brandishes the shard of ice in front of her, facing the fifty pairs of eyes shining in the darkness.

The hound gives a savage howl, and all fifty elemental spirits move at once.

She squeezes her eyes shut, waiting for the claws, the teeth…

They do not come.

She opens her eyes.

The hounds are nowhere to be seen.

The pink-robed elemental spirit leans against a tree, looking utterly spent. She reaches out to hold him, but he is too heavy for her to support and they both sink onto the grass.

What happened? she asks.

I sent them to another dimension, he says, his voice barely above a whisper.

Sent them to another dimension? What does that mean? Could it be… Her hand flies to her lips.

She wants the pink-robed elemental spirit to live. But that doesn't mean she wants fifty spirits to die. She pushes him away, feeling sickness well up in her stomach.

He lies on the grass, staring at her.

You are truly strange, you know, he says, as though reading her thoughts. Don't worry, they're not dead. I've sent them far away along a dimensional tunnel. It will be some time before they get out, as they have not grasped the workings of the dimensions. They are very swift on their *thousand-li feet*, though, he says wonderingly. Even though I can manipulate dimensions, they are always just a little behind...

He stops talking and closes his eyes, his kohl-black lashes heavy against his cheeks.

Hey, she says, bending over him to tap him on his other shoulder, so as to avoid having to shake the blood-soaked one.

I'm all right, he whispers, his whole body still except for his lips. I just need to force this poison out before it goes any further.

The crimson patch on his shoulder makes the pallor on his face all the more pronounced. His sleeping face is the perfect picture of guilelessness. She is unused to this vulnerable side of him. Lying on the grass, all the tension seems to have left his body, reminding her with a pang of a broken zither string. After the events of the night, she just wants to sleep. He said the hounds will not be back, but she ought to stay and keep watch, just in case. She has not spent the night outdoors before. The only jungle she has been in is a concrete one. She draws her knees up against her chest, preparing for a long, lonesome vigil.

She doesn't know when she falls asleep, but when she wakes up, the sun is rising above the mountains in the distance. Her robes are covered in dew and drool – much to her mortification. The elemental spirit has awoken and is looking at her with his disconcertingly direct gaze. She wipes the saliva from her face, blushing. *Looks like his lordship is back*, she thinks. She wonders when those lashes ever lowered for anyone. Probably never.

Why didn't you wake me? she says.

He continues staring at her, until she squirms under his gaze.

Why haven't you left?

Watching out for you, she says, indignation making her uncharacteristically outspoken. You could thank me.

His eyebrows arch.

Thank you? What do I have to thank you for?

She sighs and gets up, brushing the blades of grass off her clothes. I should get back to the academy now. You have a good day, she says.

He rises from the grass.

Lead us to a clean source of water, he commands. I need to wash.

What?

I said, lead—

I know what you said.

They stand for a few moments looking at each other. This elemental spirit is clearly used to getting what he wants, exactly the way he wants it. Since she sees no way of getting out of it, she decides to go along with it. Hasn't she already stayed the whole night? She may as well stay for bath time, too. She can continue to resist or try to make a break for it, but that would mean fighting against or running away from an elemental spirit who can open a portal or freeze your limbs off with just a stare. Besides, he saved her life – not that she would have been in danger, if not for him.

The mirror-like lake is all sky and iridescence, the kind of vision one dreams about but never actually experiences. Oft-mentioned by the male students, swimming in it is like falling into the sky.

She presents it with a flourish, irrationally proud, as though it's hers. In a way, it is.

The elemental spirit tosses her his outer robe and wades in. Wash this, he says. His wet inner robe clings to his body.

She has seen many naked torsos, on screen and on magazine spreads. But this is the best torso she has ever seen. Effortless is the word. All the models she has encountered, both human and CG, appear contrived. The 3D models are laboured over, of course, whereas the human models look like they tried too hard. His is a grace entirely natural and all the more difficult to attain because of it. Just think of make-up that attempts to look like it is not there, or surgeries that strive to efface their own traces.

He catches her staring at him and stretches, before turning his back on her, smirking. If she could blush to the tips of her hair, she would. She's about to tell him he can wash his own clothes, when she sees the wound on his shoulder.

It has not healed. If anything, a dark corona has spread under his skin; the blood around the wound is a viscid black. Her heart twists. It is like seeing black rot chewing up a pristine lotus.

Chuckling at her silence, he turns back to look at her. Their eyes meet and, in that instant, her concern seems naked, obscene. She ducks her eyes, suddenly busy with washing his garment. He turns away and finishes washing himself in silence.

When he comes up to the shore, they sit on opposite sides of the fire he ordered she light, his garment drying on a makeshift stand of twigs between them, so they are hidden from each other. The elemental spirit is oddly morose. Another thing she has noticed: everything about him tends to be dramatic. She still does not know his identity for sure, but he certainly seems to be somebody with status, or at least accustomed to being treated as such. When he is affronted, he displays it, presumably as somebody would soon be scrambling to appease him. When he is pleased, his face fills with the spring wind, like it is described in the lyric poem 'Qin Yuan Chun' (沁园春), 'Spring in the Water Garden'. When he is melancholic, as he is now, he brings to life the image of the lone figure sitting in a city of sadness, as recounted in the letter by Han general Li Ling to Su Wu (答苏武书). She stifles a giggle, picturing him. *Ow!* A pebble hits the toe of her shoe, the only part of her visible from behind the makeshift curtain.

He picks up his drying outer robe and puts it over himself, the crimson patch on his shoulder now a watered rose. She cannot contain her smile at his lamentable appearance.

What are you so happy about? he grouses.

Nothing, she says.

She can almost hear him thinking, *lunatic.*

The time has come for them to part. They dawdle on each side of the twig fence. She can't help but feel a little sad, knowing they will probably not meet again. After all, they have been through some things together.

It is her who speaks first. I'm going back now. If you're ever near the academy, come and visit. Take care, will you?

There, she has extended the invitation to him. She does not think he will ever visit, but there is no harm in asking.

I'll go with you, he says. To the academy.

You don't have to, she says, regretting the words as soon as they leave her mouth. He won't withdraw his offer, will he?

I have some business with your principal.

He can't be referring to Master Hai Tao (海涛) – Master Wave – who is never seen around the academy, can he? Who does not teach, but spends the day holed up in his office. How do they know each other?

I see, she says. Although she does not see at all.

They walk along the mountain path, the elemental spirit lagging behind. She wonders why he is walking so slowly. Do his wounds hurt? She sneaks worried glances over her shoulder, until she ascertains that, aside from the brooding expression on his face, he seems to be completely fine and is walking with no difficulty she can see.

They reach the Vermillion Gate.

A few students are sweeping the courtyard. Eyebrows are raised when they see the pair of them approaching: in recognition, due to her sudden fame around the academy; in amazement, at their dishevelled appearance; in wonderment, at the literally brooding good looks of her companion. The elemental spirit stops outside the gate.

Aren't you coming in? she asks.

After you, he says.

She shrugs and steps through the gate, which blazes vermillion.

She steps out.

The gate lights up again. Incandescent even in daylight.

Her jaw drops.

The elemental spirit takes in all of this, a look of resignation on his face.

Then he steps through the gate himself.

It flashes for him, too.

紅塵

Red Dust

15

The glint of teeth, of claws, in the moonlight. Her eyes squeezed shut; except the ripping of teeth and claws did not come. She had positioned herself between him and the army of hounds. The icy dagger trembled in her hand, stained a bright red. She saw their faces as if she had floated out of herself, in a strange gapless instance, far away and close up at the same time – the hound's shocked, his pale and gasping, hers stricken. The resident orchestra within herself kept up the mournful soundtrack.

She was going away to a secluded hotel for the weekend. To entice guests in spite of its distance from the city's centre, the hotel was modelled after a *kampong* – villages the first settlers lived in. The last one had long been demolished by the time she was born. The chalets had sloping roofs, with sunshades of aluminium mimicking attap thatching. A small room off the side of the main lobby functioned as a museum, where people could view framed photographs and a quaint model of a village. The receptionist handing her the key card roused her from her daydream.

People also came to this hotel in search of sleep. Judging from the complimentary sleep mask on her pillow, the hotel was aware of this tangential reputation. Sleepers came with their jammies, teddies and *chou chous* – pillows filled with dried bean sprout husks, sewn by grandmothers and laid on drowsing newborn grandchildren. Their dry whisperings whenever the infant stirs are said to prevent the baby from being startled. People also found the *kampong*-style food served at the restaurant to be comforting before they headed off to rest. Unfortunately, their signature dish was unavailable.

'The farm across the causeway, which provides the *kampong* chicken, has ceased operations. We're still looking for another supplier. Would you like to try the plant-based chicken instead? Made from jackfruit, a ubiquitous *kampong* tree.'

Her colleagues must have been heading into the theatre, for Jacq had posted a picture of the team posing in front of the anime poster in the group chat. Minus Alex, who had stayed home to work on his insectile zombie film. He would like to make the deadline this year, if possible, now that the holographic installation project was over. But in his last message, in the morning, he mentioned that his baby daughter seemed to have caught the stomach flu and had been throwing up. They must have used Jacq's phone, but Nick was the one taking the picture so she could pose with her hands in her pockets, body angled like slanted sunlight. Jayson had responded with a red, pulsing heart.

When the room service arrived, she thought about her exchange with Jacq when she had declined the invitation; she took the dish to the balcony and sent the photo, *sans* human, to the group chat. *Enjoy the movie. Sorry to miss this one.*

She ate the stir-fried jackfruit pieces in bed – something she would never do at home. Hotels always bring out another person in people, like dreams. The screen on the wall babbled like a second person in the room. Instead of energy, she imagined the food releasing lethargy.

The baths in the hotel were electrically, not geothermally, heated. A projection of a snowy bamboo grove, soft snow tracing arabesques through the air, gave the impression of being in a *rotenburo*, or open-air bath, but the effect was somewhat spoilt by

'4minsbamboo.mov' appearing at the start of each loop. Since icy air was in short supply unless produced by an air conditioner, the ice bath was actually more comforting. Unlike the steaming bath, which was in perpetual motion, the cold bath was completely still. The trick was to lie there without moving – flowing water conducts heat away from the body – until a layer of warmth built up between skin and water.

A mother and child entered, and soon the child was shrieking and running around the bath. The scar on the woman's abdomen indicated that the birth had been a C-section. She returned to her room, shutting the door on the mother crying out to the child to be careful on the wet floors.

As she idly tapped through travel vlogs featuring the hotel, Empi suggested that a sleep stream going on right at this moment might be of interest. The streamer, jolynnbaby, was apparently at the same resort. She tapped on the notification, which took her to EmpiLive. The streamer was lying down in a room like hers. She recognised the palm-print wallpaper, the carved pineapple finials on the headboard. The audience was keeping her up, trying to find out her room number. The sugar dusting of blush on her cheeks made them look like peaches. Her upturned throat was the underbelly white of a fish. Did she apply powder there as well? It was difficult to tell because of the underwater lighting set-up. jolynnbaby bantered with her viewers, and she was enthralled by the ease with which the streamer kept the conversation aloft. It was like watching a skilled juggler, or a tennis player. She found herself drafting some greetings. *Hi.* How uninspired. *Hello everyone.* Too ebullient. *What's up?* Is anyone even going to respond to that?

I am in the same hotel, she finally typed. She got the *Radioactive Wand* for her avatar, which made her words glow, so she stood out in the sea of rapidly scrolling text.

'Serious? What a coincidence!' jolynnbaby said.

The popular internet celebrity chatted with her for the next thirty seconds, asking after her day and why she was there. Her heart fluttered within her chest. She donated $49.99. *Try the chicken*, she typed. *It's good. Although it's jackfruit instead of chicken today.*

jolynnbaby ordered the chicken for dinner. 'I didn't get to sleep a wink because of you guys!' The other participants tried to get her to stake out to see which room the staff delivered the chicken to. She was almost overwhelmed by the attention. What did she do, except be at the right place at the right time? She decided to try the *ikan kembung* – just like how Mom makes it! – although her mother had never made anything like that. Some users shared what they were having for dinner. She suspected those who exhibited the more exotic food, like balut and the stargazy pie, did it for effect – although she already knew about those dishes because they were such frequent candidates for sensation.

Love in the Snow *starting in 4 mins*, someone typed.

Penultimate week. So sad.

'Shall we watch it together?' said the streamer.

Detective Kang had finally realised Josie Wong was a thousand-year-old nine-tailed fox. In fact, their paths had crossed even earlier: she had rescued him when he was a young boy (wrong turn down an alleyway, man with scar on right hand). Life was filled with sidereal symmetries; the boy she saved would in turn save her many years later. Adding to the tangled web of fate, the serial killer the detective was pursuing was actually the man from the alleyway all those years ago, *and* a ten-thousand-year-old evil spirit, *and* the nine-tailed fox's age-old enemy. Detective Kang's eyes, wide with disbelief, filled the screen. Josie's long silvery hair fluttered in the wind – then stopped moving. *You are my destiny. A destiny like the fallen snow.* She sighed.

Why isn't there anyone like Detective Kang at my local police station? someone wrote.

Because he would be on perma-administrative leave for firing his gun every episode, someone replied.

'Oooh, that's a good one,' said Jolynn.

Someone was trying to garner support for a petition to save the forest.

'You mean the one that's gonna be bulldozed to make way for another development of shoebox apartments? I should go for a walk, huh? Before it happens.'

She was a disembodied ghost eavesdropping on multiple strands of conversation. Here and there, she would respond with a quip. Somewhere along the way, she subscribed. Spectating a conversation always had the effect of putting her to sleep. The feeling of calm was like watching something exploding from a safe distance.

Red Dust

16

She opened her eyes and saw her rumpled image on the wall-mounted screen. The palm-print wallpaper, accents of white and tan in addition to details of cane and wicker, gave the impression of a colonial paradise. A steamer trunk – decorative – sat in the corner of the room.

The dream world had never displayed such discontinuity before. Where was the Vermillion Gate? The paisley patterns on the armchair looked just as irregular. Prior to today, she had not seen paisley anywhere in the dream world.

She shot up.

Her phone, still connected by its umbilical cord to the panel on the headboard, clattered onto the carpeted floor. It was like four muffled thuds on the door of unhappiness. The same door that opened for Meursault that fateful day on the beach in Camus's *The Stranger.*

She had woken up in a strange place. She tried to quiet the rising tumult in her chest. There must be an explanation to this. Perhaps she did not manage to enter into a dream state? She couldn't have done anything to lose her access to the dream world, could she?

Then she remembered the disc. She had left it at home.

Throughout the journey to her flat, she felt like someone had taken her insides and scrambled them. The cab seemed to be going through a time loop, traversing through the same kilometres of similitude over and over again.

Her door, usually so familiar, seemed different, like a door of judgement. The handle whispered its sentence to her fingers when she pressed on it. The walk to her bedroom seemed to take more steps than usual, as though more tiles were unrolling under her feet, like a carpet. She feared she would not find the cube in the drawer. After all, everything was uncommon today. Perhaps her nightstand would no longer be the same nightstand. But it was there, a triangle of light falling from the curtain to rest along an edge. The cube split itself into two like it was spilling its secrets. As usual, the sight of it defying gravity sent a shock wave through the quotidian. The disc was inside, monumental in its perfection, stark against its setting of brilliant white, presenting itself in full force for perception. *I am here*, it seemed to be saying to her. It did not turn on but winked in the light when she held it, as if assuring her it was alive.

Do you consent to enter into a parallel universe?

She cradled the cube in the cab all the way back to the hotel, her fingers stroking its smudge-proof surfaces, clutching at its solidity. She did not know when she had started directing her supplications to the featherlight weight on her lap.

Please, let me go back.

I'll never doubt you again, if you let me go back.

Academy of Greatest Learning

17

Even the White Dragon, who already turned heads wherever he went, felt he needed more attention, to be known even more.

What other purpose was there for him to create a *luminous* gate?

In addition, he could not be the only one for whom the gate glowed. No, that would have been too narcissistic. The spotlight must always be shared – with a lesser being who would never be able to steal it.

Not a single broom in the courtyard is moving now. Everyone has given up all pretences of sweeping.

The gate had glowed for Grandmaster Chao Ying because the Ice Dragon made her a co-founder. But why is it glowing for *her*? It has never done so before.

Th-There's something wrong with this gate, she stammers. I'm not the founder...

You're not, but I am, the elemental spirit says.

She thinks back to the way he had chilled the morning air, the day when she first met him.

How he had frozen the senior student's hand.

How he could conjure ice out of thin air.

This elemental spirit really is the Ice Dragon.

Xue Long, the Ice Dragon.

Still, something doesn't make sense.

You may be, she says, but me, I'm not.

The Ice Dragon sighs. All the privileges I have are yours, too, by *contract*. That also includes *immortality*. A mere *gate* is hardly worth fussing over.

Contract? Immortality? This is almost too much to take. He can't mean the summoning contract, right? When did that happen? Did he not say he had no intention of making a contract with her, that last night was the last she would ever see of him?

Last night must be when it happened.

Last night, the gate was still behaving normally when she walked under it. It was this morning when it started to behave strangely.

Now, we go and see your principal, he says, jolting her out of her confused thoughts. Lead the way.

Because she is still stunned, she forgets to ask why she should be guiding. It isn't that she's unwilling – he's the guest, after all. Under normal circumstances, she would be glad to accompany him. She had even invited him to visit, before. It is his tone that makes her feel like throwing him to somebody else, starting from the seniors who kidnapped her – it's just that they are nowhere to be found.

She is also unsure about where she will find Master Wave's office, because she has never needed to see him before. It seems that no one has: the students she stops to ask for directions are similarly clueless. By now, they have attracted quite a following, the greater part of them female. The Ice Dragon is as calm as ever, apparently used to such attention.

Still haven't figured it out? he asks.

She grits her teeth.

At length, a whey-faced student points a trembling finger at an elevated building in the distance, at the highest point of the academy. Evidently, the principal likes the penthouse.

The office is located at the farthest corner of the sprawling campus. They start in its general direction, keeping it in sight like a distant star. Sometimes the path they are following leads to a dead end and they have to retrace their steps. Sometimes it veers off suddenly into another direction and they have to decide whether to keep following it, hoping it will eventually right itself again. Their little party soon takes to calling from the bridge where they are standing, or from the fork in the pathway ahead, actively taking part in finding the way with them. It is proving to be an arduous journey, but the girls do not seem to mind. Suddenly, she has a brilliant idea.

Why don't I leave you with them? she says to the Ice Dragon. I'm sure, collectively, they can do a better job than me.

The Ice Dragon looks at her with a gaze frigid enough to bring about the next Pleistocene.

Finally, they stand under a steep flight of stone steps up a cliff face, snaking towards heaven. At its zenith perches the building that is the rumoured office of the principal.

We'll leave you now, the girls beam.

Thank you for your help, she says.

The Ice Dragon acknowledges them with a tilt of his head. A tilt that sends many hearts lurching.

They begin their ascent, leaving the fluttering hearts behind. The female students linger until he is completely out of sight, their faces becoming indistinct, obscured by a thin layer of mist, as though seen through the veil of a *weimao*. She is reminded of the first impression she had of the academy, that it was built for an avian race. They are hardly halfway up before she is gasping for breath. If only all the exercise she gets here could be accrued to her waking life. The Ice Dragon steps on her heels. When she turns around to glare at him, he just grins at her.

After what seems like an eternal climb, they finally stand before the door of Master Wave's eyrie. Can the principal of a school be such a recluse? Surely there must be an overwhelming number of administrative tasks awaiting his handling. But then, she is not a particularly communicative administrator herself.

She raps the lion-headed knocker against the wooden door. Something clatters on the floor inside. She waits, but nobody comes to the door.

Master Hai Tao? she calls.

Something else crashes, followed by the hesitant sound of a chair scraping. There is the sound of a bolt being drawn. The door opens.

A young man, dressed in white cotton robes that look like pyjamas, stands in the doorway, his black hair in a topknot. His skin is fair like rice milk. There is a softness and gentleness about him: if the jade rabbit had an incarnation, it would look a lot like him. Come to think of it, the jade rabbit lives on the moon, too.

Hello, she greets him. We're looking for Master Hai Tao. Is he in?

I am Hai Tao, the young man says.

This academy is filled with strange things, but the strangest of all has got to be this principal who looks like he has only recently left the cradle. *Lanuginous* comes to her mind. She stares at him until the Ice Dragon clears his throat behind her.

I'm sorry, she says. It's just that you look so young...

He grins, showing an even set of small white teeth.

It's okay, I get that a lot. Come on in.

The entrance opens immediately into an office. Bookshelves line three walls, except the wall directly opposite the door, which is lined with windows. This is where the principal's overflowing desk is placed. The Ice Dragon goes to the only chair in the room – behind the desk – and sits down.

Why didn't you come out to receive us? Is the jade mirror broken?

She decides it is better for her to intervene at this point.

This is Xue Long, she explains. He is an Ice Dragon.

The Ice Dragon, he says, his expression darkening. There's only one of me.

She gulps.

The principal turns to her, smiling. I know the founder.

Then he turns back to the elemental spirit and continues, Pardon me. The jade mirror isn't broken. Although I almost broke it, when it lit up. I thought there had been a mistake. I wasn't expecting to meet the Ice Dragon in my lifetime.

This is the first time they're meeting? What business do they have to discuss?

The Ice Dragon looks slightly mollified. Some of the spring wind returns to the deep dark of his eyes. She lets out a breath she did not realise she has been holding.

Allow me to go and change, says Master Wave. As you can probably tell by now, I seldom get visitors.

He disappears into an adjacent room, probably his living quarters. While he is gone, she surveys the mess on the floor. There is an upended brazier, its contents – what looks like agarwood – scattered on the floor. That must be the first clatter she heard when she knocked. A few feet away is a pile of books that must have belonged to the tower of volumes on the crowded desk and an overturned inkstone. The spilled black ink could be passed off as *action painting* in her world.

When the principal reappears, he is dressed in the white-over-blue robes of the masters of the academy, except his inner robe is dark instead of pale blue.

Thank you for waiting, says Master Wave. What is it that has brought the White Dragon to the academy?

This student here, the Ice Dragon says, indicating her with his gaze, will be serving me from now on. She will be leaving the academy today.

What?

I see... Master Wave says.

She turns to the Ice Dragon. You did not clear this with me. I'm not going anywhere.

Master Wave clears his throat.

Uh… It seems as though the student is not willing.

Xue Long looks at her as if she were particularly slow-witted. You don't seem to have grasped the situation. You don't have a choice.

She sees the prison bars bearing down upon her, hears the clink of the shackles. For a moment, she can only look at him in a kind of helpless amazement. *No*. She does not have to contend with that. Not here. Life may be severe, unyielding. But this is not Life.

Sorry to have bothered you, she tells the principal. Please disregard everything that has been said. She glares at the Ice Dragon and walks out of the room.

Master Wave goes to the door and calls after her, There's no need to climb all the way up here to see me. Just borrow a jade mirror from any one of the masters next time.

Is that how the principal handles the day-to-day running of the academy? Video conferencing? Through a jade mirror? This would make management tolerable even for the most withdrawn administrator. She should look into testing something similar on her colleagues.

She has not yet advanced ten paces before she hears the Ice Dragon behind her.

There's no way you can stay at the academy, he says. Think about who will be after you. The dimensional tunnel will not hold the hounds forever.

It's you they're after, she says, not me.

They'll be after you, from now on.

She turns to face him. Why is that?

For the first time, he looks put on the spot. She watches as a number of complicated emotions play across his face, like clouds skimming across the surface of water. It is obvious there are things he does not want to admit to her, to himself even, things he would like to keep her in the dark about, if he can.

She decides she needs to provoke him, if she is ever going to learn the truth.

I'm your master now, right?

His eyebrows lift, outrage colouring his countenance like plum blossoms in snow. People usually look flushed and florid when they are angry, but not him.

You couldn't even let them harm a single hair on my head, she presses. You were being pursued, but still you had to come. You couldn't leave until you had taken care of them.

He quickly regains his composure.

If I were you, he says, his voice light as snowfall, I would keep the events of the night secret, hidden away, deep in my heart. I would not even say it out loud. You never know who might be listening. I would not speak so casually, I am a *dragon's master.*

The blossoms have withered away now, replaced by layers of impenetrable snow.

I would try to forget I was even there. I would try to bury any trace of my being there. Because there are many who dream of the power of dragons and they will do *anything* to obtain that power through me.

All that he says is true, she realises. He rescued her easily enough from four weak human beings. Even against fifty elemental spirits, he managed to preserve them both. He is very strong. But she is an easy target. One of these days, an attempt to take her out would be sure to succeed.

As if echoing her thoughts, he continues, I can't have my weak point running around, can I?

Can't we just forget this? she suggests. I'll stay out of trouble. You won't have to appear around me again. I'll live my life, and you live yours.

Can you really? You already seem to be the target of your schoolmates. I can only guess why...

He is annoyingly astute. She wonders if anything ever slips past him.

At least a dozen students saw what happened at the Vermillion Gate this morning, and a dozen more followed you on your trek through the academy. Do you really think you can stay out of trouble?

She thinks about it long and hard. *Probably not.*

Yes, she answers.

She turns and walks away.

What is it you like so much about this academy? he asks. There are far better places you've never seen before.

I'm not sure, she says. It's just that there's so much I don't know about this world. I want to learn about it slowly, my way. Not get swept up in things not of my own choosing. *Like in my real life,* she thinks.

That's it? I can teach you. I'm the one who taught your Grandmaster everything.

She stops so suddenly he almost collides with her. She whirls around to face him.

Do you mean that?

You should address me as 'Master', as you call your teachers at the academy.

You'll really teach me? She gazes at him for a long time, at the corners of his lips, lifted in what appears to be a guileless smile.

Can I leave tomorrow instead? I would like to say goodbye to my friends.

He pauses, and she thinks he might object.

Tomorrow morning, at the latest.

She claps both hands to her mouth to contain her glee and he grins, more convincingly this time, dazzling like the sun.

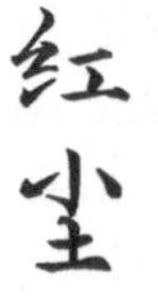

Red Dust

18

The bedside control panel told her it was 4.04pm. She felt refreshed, like a new person. Whatever renewal processes that occurred while she slept had erased the jangled nerves, the swollen lymph nodes, the sourness in her stomach.

Now she had ascertained that the disc was the source of her dreams, she was desperate to find out more about it. But there was nothing: no news item, no information at all on a 'device that enables parallel universe travel'. No one was talking about it on any Empi community either. The only thing she could do was start her own discussion, switching on a lamp to better capture the floating cube, causing it to irradiate with a certain quality of light. *Annunciation in a Hotel Room*. Something like that.

Anyone seen anything like this before? she posted, before tapping on the alert that jolynnbaby had been live for an hour.

Jolynn was having a late lunch. The streamer had checked out earlier, in the morning. She looked at the meal – slices of banana, berries, nut butter and dragon fruit sorbet on an açaí bowl in a café somewhere – and the time, had a premonition and booked a ride.

While in the cab, she scanned through the replies her post had received. *Where did you get this? It looks so cool. Looks like something from a movie. Guys, I've just taken my meds. Don't know. Are you selling it? Hope you're okay. The heck is this? DM me.*

Suddenly, she was filled with an overwhelming impulse to take down the post. Why had she even shared it? Was she curious about the origin of the dream-travelling device? Yes. But not as curious as to risk having it taken away from her. What if the package had not been intended for her? By a stroke of luck, it had ended up on her doorstep. Obviously, its existence was not common knowledge. With so many things unknown, it was best to proceed with caution.

The driver dropped her off at the bus stop where the entrance to the forest was. By now, she had realised what a foolhardy plan it was. The streamer had mentioned her desire to visit so she had assumed she was going to do it. All because of Jolynn's choice of lunch and the vespertine hour – people hike in the mornings and evenings to escape the sun's glare.

She could have gone to the café but that would not have been artful. No, she would have to be chanced upon, waiting from the future, to be welcomed. The wait would have been sufferable if not for the mosquitos. Everyone knows the sound they make is worse than their bite.

Jolynn appeared to be wandering aimlessly, hopping to another café for its speciality iced coconut water Americano, then sipping it as she chose a candy bar from a convenience store. She was about to acknowledge she had made a mistake when Jolynn boarded the bus which passed through her stop. Everyone tried to guess where she was going. Her hands shook as she typed.

Where I am?

'Where are you?' Jolynn said.

She took a video of her surroundings.

'No way…'

Something like a fuzzy yellow light bulb switched on inside her, flooding her with light.

'Guys, this is too coincidental.'

The chat exploded.

The fuzzy yellow feeling spread through her, emanating from her pores, her breath, so the little road was bathed in liquid light that had nothing to do with the fluorescence of the early evening sun. The entire landscape became miraculous. Every curve, every blade of grass, was affected. The whine of the mosquitos subsided into an agitated humming in the air, vibrating with the spirited surroundings.

Yet the feeling evaporated as quickly as it came. As Jolynn's bus advanced closer to her stop, bringing the streamer like a prophecy, a shining vision, a bright sign, disquiet began to rise in her. Should she be lying in wait, a mantis with forelegs raised in prayer, for her prey to arrive? If she overstayed her welcome, the coincidences would no longer be seen as pleasurable. She might as well be holding a placard waiting for an idol to arrive. Besides, what would she do when Jolynn appeared? Wave and shake hands? Would her paw be found too hot, too cold, too clammy? Perhaps she would be caught on the livestream sidling up towards the streamer, dazed smile, awkward-limbed. None of these scenarios she wished to see. Best to make her getaway.

Happy hiking.

She followed the streamer slipping and sliding in the mud as she returned to the hotel, leaving the livestream at eight for *Love in the Snow*. Before the episode began, she was shown the trailers of three other shows that had just begun airing or were airing within the next couple of weeks. *Lovers in the Sun* was speculated to be an even bigger hit. The leading man was a rising star known for his 'speaking eyes'. When she rejoined the stream, Jolynn had made her way out of the forest – or not – and the broadcast had ended. She went for a soak in the baths one last time, before she had to check out in the morning, and then laid out the set of work clothes she had packed so she could leave for the office directly from the hotel. Recovering the post she had taken down, she played back the video of the cube she had taken earlier, watching it float like a celestial messenger in a cloud of tungsten incandescence. Her finger hovered over the upload button.

In the end, she just had to know. In spite of everything.

Academy of Greatest Learning

19

Although they live next to each other, and have known each other since the first day she arrived at the academy, this is the first time she is in Brilliant Jade's room. She is surprised by the decor, thinking it will be identical to hers, with its wood and lacquered surfaces. Certainly, the furniture is the same: there is the cabinet with the painted landscape on it, but it is an autumn scene, instead of the spring scene in her room – these cabinets must have originally been a pair. The writing desk is also the same, with the stationary box on top of it. The bed, too, and the mirrored stand, although their placements in the room differ.

But that is where all similarities end. The feel of her friend's room is entirely different, due in no small part to the fact that it is overflowing with boy band-themed merchandise. The autumn landscape cabinet has become a display shelf for the *chibi* versions of the band members. They wink and blow kisses at her from a thousand posters covering every inch of the wall. The bedspread is printed with a life-sized, bare-chested photo of a doe-eyed, milky-skinned youth, probably her bias of the group, with cherry lips and longish hair, escaping tendrils curling around the base of his neck. The pillow bears the same image of the head, so his face will not be obscured when the pillow is placed on the bed, and most importantly, so the sleeper's face can be next to the idol's.

You know FLWR? Brilliant Jade says, catching her marvelling at the contrast between the quiet darkness of the black lacquered bed frame and the gaudiness of the digitally printed sheets.

I guess you wouldn't like the furnishings provided by the academy, huh? she observes. Virtually every trace of sombreness has been submerged under a cheerful high-key palette.

They're okay, Brilliant Jade says, studying her. Walking up to the golden-hued cabinet that seems to hold the very essence of autumn itself, she explains, My figurines look quite nice on them.

If you like them that way, she says. Brilliant Jade has her tastes, she has hers. Who's to argue about predilections?

Brilliant Jade is still looking at her and she meets her upturned eyes with a smile. Blinking, Brilliant Jade sits down at the low table in the centre of the room and pours out a cup of tea, motioning for her friend to take a seat next to her.

I can't believe you're leaving the academy, Brilliant Jade mutters, pushing a small dish with a glutinous rice flour cake filled with mung bean paste towards her.

Xue Long is sleeping in her room, so she will be bunking with Brilliant Jade. That way, they can spend her last night at the academy together, too.

I'll miss you, she admits to Brilliant Jade.

Ask your master to do his dimension-crossing thing so you can visit. It's easy for him, right?

I'm not sure if he'll do what I request, but I'll definitely be asking.

After she had agreed to leave with the White Dragon, they walked back up the steps to bang on the lion-headed knocker again, much to the surprise of Master Wave. The story the three of them settled on was that Xue Long is a travelling master who spied potential in her – one he alone can see – and asked to take her in as a disciple, which she accepted, so she will be leaving the academy to begin her discipleship. They surmise about half the student population will believe the story.

The other half will soon be won over, as life rearranges itself around them. The glowing gate will be seen as an aberration. How old is it anyway? As for the rest – the dimensional portal, the crackling ice, the declaration he made that day on the summoning field, 'I'm a *dragon*' – all these will have their explanations. She hopes.

Still, you must be so happy, Brilliant Jade says. I mean, all of this is just so... *right*.

What do you mean?

You've always been the one who is more into this summoning business anyway. Then all of a sudden, this master appears. I can't think of anyone more suitable for this to happen to.

That's just because worms freak you out, she teases. If the boys from FLWR could be summoned, you'd lock yourself in the crafting room day and night!

Just before nightfall, she leaves Brilliant Jade's room and makes her way to Master Dawn's cabin.

I've been expecting you, says Master Dawn, gesturing to a small round mirror that had always been sitting on the sideboard but to which she'd never paid much attention. It is made of a white jade known as 'mutton fat' jade – due to its unctuousness resembling tallow. The principal says you're leaving tomorrow with a travelling master.

In the corner of the kitchen, Xi Xi has collapsed onto her bed, feigning sleep as usual. A present for you, she says, dropping a bunch of bananas next to the *You Yan*, causing the spirit to drop her pretence and snatch it up, chittering.

Just one, she says, seeing Master Dawn has produced a dish of osmanthus cakes, together with the mountain oolong. I had too many mung bean cakes.

My mirror does not light up like the principal's whenever the White Dragon comes to visit, Master Dawn says when they are both seated. But I think this Master White must be none other than Xue Long, isn't he?

How do you know? she says, astonished.

So I'm right? Master Dawn beams.

You tricked me!

Master Dawn shrugs. It all adds up. Plus, more than one student said they saw the Vermillion Gate light up this morning.

She holds a finger to her lips.

Master Dawn mirrors her gesture, smiling.

*

Travelling through a dimensional corridor is unnerving at first, like hurtling through thin air. But once you get used to the sensation of not being bound to space, the feeling is actually quite exhilarating. Like flying. The White Dragon keeps a firm grip on her hand as the world around her fades to white, reminding her of a science experiment in which a wheel is filled in with seven colours and spun. Sometimes she can make out bands of colour – mountains, pulled out of shape, or streams and ribbons of what look like forests and bodies of water. She reaches out.

Don't, he says, smacking her hand, if you don't want to get lost between dimensions.

She lets her hand fall hurriedly and contents herself with looking. Every day in this world is filled with new experiences. She peers at the floating colours around her. None of the terrains whizzing by her are familiar, and that is only to be expected. Dimension-bending distortion aside, her low level of summoning skills hardly allowed her to venture very far from the academy.

Here we are, he says.

The whiteness breaks up as they slow down, coalescing into clumps of snow. They are in an icy bamboo grove. The whole landscape is blanketed in white. Snow is falling, all around her. So this is the Bathing Snow Forest (沐雪林), abode of the White Dragon and the legendary cradle of the summoning world. Chao Ying mentioned it in her book, but not even the Grandmaster had set foot in it. Vermillion lanterns glow against the elemental half-light, the blue of aerial spaces, lighting up a path to the mouth of a cave. The hushed bamboo forest has the atmosphere of an inner sanctum. She is star-struck. Her awe must be obvious: Xue Long looks at her face and chuckles.

She looks at him, standing against the backdrop of sprightly bamboo trees. Bamboo is supposed to epitomise the gentleman; she has no doubt he was aware of this when he chose to set up house in a bamboo grove. Bamboo defies the frost, flexible yet unyielding in the face of adversity – although for the Ice Dragon, frost is not something to be resisted as much as commanded. The hollow stem of the bamboo is akin to the modest heart of the gentleman in accepting instruction – although there is nothing modest about the Ice Dragon, from all she has seen. Funny how arrogance is constructed as being full of oneself, as if it is better to be porous, allow others in.

The graceful appearance of the bamboo has often been used to extol the comeliness of a gentleman as early as in one of the odes of Wei in the *Classic of Poetry*. In 'Qi Riverbend' (卫风·淇奥), each of the three stanzas describing the character, appearance and poise of the gentleman is preceded by the lush imagery of bamboo. This is probably the only – and she suspects, to him, the most important – part of the extended metaphor that applies to Xue Long, with his graceful bearing, his fluid movements that make everyone else appear ungainly next to him.

They walk down the lantern-lit path until they arrive at the entrance of the cave, which she thinks, at first, they will have to pass through. *Through caverns measureless to man.* Except instead of a sunless sea, it will lead to a palatial dwelling in the middle of nowhere. Her idea of cave dwelling is limited to pop culture depictions of Cro-Magnons roasting a hog on a spit. She cannot imagine him doing that, in his white robes.

Except the cave turns out to be his home.

She gawks. The place is... cavernous. It is completely hewn out of a frosty, softly luminescent jade, like the one that takes seven years to be dug out from under thousands of feet of ice and snow in a Jin Yong novel. The ceiling arches heavenward until it is lost in shadow. Every piece of furniture is chiselled out of the jadeite rock face. Rising up from the floor in the middle of the room – or hall, more like – is the Bed. It is an elaborate affair. There is no mistaking the hierarchy of activities, what he likes to do most, where he prefers spending his time. It seems like all the comfort is concentrated here. The bedding is soft and downy, like a heap of snow. The covers are woven with a silky, pearlescent thread so it glimmers with rainbows at the slightest movement, like fish scales, or the scales on a butterfly's wings. This makes her feel somewhat mournful as she searches for a place to string her hammock.

There is a table in the far corner. Only one chair, she notes. This is the ultimate bachelor pad, or man cave. But he is not a man. And she feels out of place. She is beginning to regret leaving her room and her friends at the academy to come here.

He makes a beeline – dragon's line – for the Bed.

Aren't you supposed to be teaching me useful skills? she protests.

That is why she has agreed to leave the academy in the first place. Instead of responding, he simply disappears under the covers.

There is nothing to be done. She has no sway over him, although technically he is the servant and she the master, by a phenomenal twist of fate. But even the thought of it is almost sacrilegious. She has accepted, too eagerly in hindsight. She could have thought about it more, laid down some terms or conditions, perhaps. Whether he would have abided by them was another thing altogether, but she needed not have snapped up the bait he had dangled in front of her so readily. She sighs to herself. Actually, it is unlikely she could ever win against the likes of someone as crafty as him.

She leaves him snoozing in his jadeite lair and steps back out into the forest. If this is to be her new home, she may as well familiarise herself with it. As she walks through the crystalline world, the snow sparkling softly under her feet in the twilight, her spirits lift. By the time she stumbles upon a crop of mushrooms, like many wayfarers in crepuscular forests, she is more ready to try to come to terms with her circumstances. They luminesce when she brushes against them, auroras coruscating across their milk-white surfaces. If not for the show of lights, she would have missed them, camouflaged in the snow. As a child, she had loved brushing against mimosa plants and watching their leaflets fold up.

A shadow falls.

She turns and finds herself face to face with the cold glint of a knife. Uselessly, she remembers she has just watched a similar scene unfolding not too long ago. She hears the background vocals in her head, the soulful music accompanying the pivotal scene she and countless viewers had replayed over and over again throughout the week, waiting for the next episode. A curious thing, how random one's thoughts can be at critical moments.

The owner of the hand pointing the blade at her has long silvery hair down to his waist. His eyes are also alarmingly silver. She does not need to see the nine tails to know this is a Nine-Tailed Fox, *whose cries are like a human baby's*. Oh shush!

It is disconcerting that another part of her, somewhere detached from herself, is thrilled that a *Nine-Tailed Fox* is standing in front of her. The other time when she had felt this way was when Xue Long appeared in the summoning field, descending from the sky, robes billowing, white like the sun reflecting off snow, just as Chao Ying had described. She had been beyond awed. She thought if she died right there, she would not have any regrets. Only... she did not die. And if she did not die then, she does not want to die now.

The Nine-Tailed Fox grins rakishly at her.

Come with me, little one.

His voice chimes. Like bells. Like silver.

It is only in this world anyone will call her 'little one'. She is definitely beyond the pale of any suggestion of diminutiveness, in her world.

She is falling through a trapdoor, a sinkhole. As she is being whisked away, she wonders if she will just disappear, like mist, or an echo. Even spiders leave traces of their silk, crickets their trails. But for her, there will be nothing, not even an impression in the snow.

Red Dust

20

'Are you all right?' Jacq asked.

She looked up slowly from her screen, not that she had been paying particular attention to what was on it.

'Yes?'

'You look out of it today. Well, you always look somewhat out of it, but particularly so today.'

'Really?'

'Yep, you've had this frown on your face since morning.'

'I'm all right.'

'You sure?'

'Yeah.'

'Okay then.'

She had been thinking. What would happen if she died in the dream world? Would the dreams stop? She knew experiences like pain, cold and tiredness work differently in dreams from the waking world. In a dream, the brain suspends disbelief. If you get scratched, or if you get stabbed, perhaps your mind's eye will let you see blood, perhaps not. But you'd know you had been stabbed. The brain has its own way of rationalising things, its own logic – the logic of dreams, which only needs to be consistent with the dream's narrative. People do not usually feel pain in dreams; things like pain and loud noise will usually wake people up – it is a basic survival mechanism, which is why people pinch themselves when they need assurance that what they are experiencing is not a dream. Still, although it is not real, the shock of it is real, which is why nightmares keep people from falling asleep. She was certain that getting stabbed, or eaten by *the extremely savage, man-eating Nine-Tailed Fox* was definitely something she did not want to experience. Granted, there was nothing savage about the refined appearance of her captor, but she knew malevolence came in all sorts of forms, even overtly genteel ones.

When did her concerns of the dreams recurring shade into concerns of the dreams actually stopping, when she would be wakened by human voices and drown? She had told no one about the shadow world – not that she had anyone she could confide in, who would incline an ear towards her like a confessional priest with auricles in his heart for the contrite. Deep down, she sensed a fragility that could be dashed by even the slightest hint of light. It was a night world, a world of adumbrations that could only be apprehended murkily, with apprehension, in the dark chambers of the heart, not examined too closely. It echoed, it was full of hollow spaces, so she must keep herself suspended if she was afraid of falling – suspension of disbelief, or else she would fall through these gaps, these holes in logic. As the dreams continued, she even felt the dream world was more substantial and the real world, its shadow – so much so that she began checking her body for the scrapes and bruises she was sure she had got. She was almost disappointed when they were not there.

She had never given serious thought about her mortality before, about life ending. Her existence might be banal, but there were some things she did not mind, like dressing up her Empi avatar and the comforting warmth of a bowl of *Mei Ling* porridge. Her only family member might be dead, but she still had people she posted birthday greetings to. If that was enough to make her cling on to the real world, all the more reason she did not want to screw up in the dream world.

It was just as well her work could be done with an elementary level of concentration. She needed to come up with a strategy to avoid dying. Though frightening, what she was most afraid of was not the gnashing of teeth, but being barred from returning to that world. But even when six thirty rolled around, she was no closer to finding a solution. Unsurprising, since she had nothing to work with – she knew nothing about her kidnapper: not his background nor inclinations, and certainly not his motives. She would have to go back, in order to find out more, and improvise. There was nothing more she could do in this world.

At the train station, she saw a stray shoe on the platform, more like a rubber sandal, really. Dark blue. Who did the stray sandal belong to? Unlike in other cities, there were no homeless people in the subways, no blankets strewn on the pavement of some street corner, with the imprint of their missing human being. The dirty old rubber sandal right in the middle of the spotless platform, spick and span like the floors of an art gallery, thus struck her as exceedingly incongruous. Like a pebble in a river obstructing the flow of water, it diverted streams of people as they skirted around to avoid it.

Little touches like these cemented reality for her. There was no reason for the sandal to be there other than the fact it was *there*. The picturesque, however, exists only if it is part of the painting. She wanted to believe the world she had access to through her dreams existed independently of her, but so far it had behaved like a world fabricated from her dreams, populated with things to her tastes. She was clearly the dreamer, in that world – nothing existed outside of herself. No sandals left behind by unknown people.

This made the dream world about as substantial as mist, because no matter how real that world might seem, furnished with details like bioluminescent mushrooms, invariably it would be met with the limits of what she could imagine, which was like a speck in the ensuing great cosmic dark.

Nights in the city were never completely silent. The sound of marbles clattering across her ceiling was something most flat dwellers would be familiar with. Various explanations had been offered – no, it wasn't that everyone was fanatical about marbles – from water hammers to metal rebars in the concrete contracting and expanding. The train rumbling past every few minutes used to bother her, but now she hardly heard it. She listened to her neighbour's children screaming. Elsewhere, a house pet barked. She put off sleep for as long as she could, but she could not put it off forever. Eventually, she had to face her spectre.

青
丘

Verdant Knoll

21

She is in a dimensional corridor, this time with the Nine-Tailed Fox.

Where are we going? she asks. *Where are you taking me?* would be the more accurate but melodramatic phrasing and, as far as possible, she wants to keep the narrative from veering in that direction.

The Nine-Tailed Fox does not reply, but keeps a firm grip on her hand.

So much for finding out about his motives.

She tries harder, fighting to keep her voice light. So, what's your name?

He cuts her off by bringing the knife close to her throat.

Shhh... His low voice is almost a croon.

Point taken.

A shift in the air current alerts her they are slowing down. The whiteness dissipates and the colours coalesce. They seem to be approaching a hilly region. *Wait. Is this...?*

Welcome to the Verdant Knoll, says the Nine-Tailed Fox, as if reading her thoughts. You have doubtless read about it.

Is it her imagination? Or is there a hint of bitterness in his voice?

They alight on grass, soft as down. She can hear the crystal tones of a stream nearby – the Fragrant Waters? So fresh, you have to stop yourself from drinking it all in order to make a summoning stone.

The Nine-Tailed Fox looks at her wide-eyed interest at their surroundings with amusement. She catches his eye and is embarrassed.

Come, he says.

He leads her to a grove of overhanging boughs, heavy with fruits an alluring red. The air is perfumed with their syrupy scent. He plucks one and hands it to her. She reaches out to take it, then hesitates.

Cautious, are we? he chuckles.

He takes a bite out of the fruit and hands her another. She reaches as if to take it, but bypasses his hand and plucks one for herself from an adjacent bough. She takes a huge bite and its juiciness floods her mouth. It tastes like a collage of all the reds in her memories. A hint of a blushing Alphonso mango she once bought and, most recently, the Tropicana fruit tea she had at the hotel.

This is good! she exclaims.

He laughs out loud.

Chomping on the fruits, they make their way to a large wooden hut almost hidden under a luxuriant growth of purple wisterias. He holds the door open for her. In the shady gloom, she makes out unaffected and cosy furnishings. A *guqin* sits in the corner, its mother-of-pearl inlay picking up a distant glimmer from the orchard outside – an exquisite specimen. From the sheen of the lacquered wood, she can tell it has been handled often. The Nine-Tailed Fox must be musically inclined. She has always thought a certain chemistry exists between a person and their keepsakes. Over time, a person's essences, so to speak, infuse into the objects and a patina forms. He pulls out a rough-hewn chair for her. She takes it, keeping him in the periphery of her vision. He sighs.

Now we wait, he says, all traces of his earlier humour gone.

The fruit in her hand has lost its taste. She sets it down quietly on the table. She looks for his knife and finds it tucked inside his sash – for now.

With the solemnity hanging over them like a giant temple bell and his eyes shut as he sits, spine ramrod straight, she almost thinks he has brought her here to meditate – except her heart is beating like a drum and the tension in the air is anything but tranquil. With the clement weather, the fragrance of wisterias in the air and the murmuring of the stream as an undertone, the sanctuary of the Nine-Tailed Foxes is a hermit's paradise. Under different circumstances, she would have enjoyed being here. But now, she takes in everything with distraction. Presently, she is drawn by a vague shimmering in the air, like a breath of wind casting ripples across the still surface of a pond.

He's here, says the Nine-Tailed Fox, his eyelashes still resting against his cheeks.

Who? she wants to ask, but the word freezes in her throat.

A layer of hoar frost creeps towards them on the floor and the balmy temperature drops by several degrees. The shimmer in the air becomes a portal and out steps the White Dragon.

Xue Long.

Kyubi.

The White Dragon shoots her a cool glance. She raises her eyebrows. The ultimate source of all this trouble is himself. She's obviously just the bait. The muscle in his left cheek quirks. He turns his attention back to the Nine-Tailed Fox.

Kyubi's eyelids flutter open. Several foxfires materialise and begin a stately dance around the room. The hoar frost recedes.

To think I'm seeing the day when you've come running to your master like a little dog, Kyubi says.

Little dog is a bit much. An overlord hunting down a runaway slave, more like.

Xue Long looks pained. You're still going on about this?

We'll never forget this! Kyubi snaps.

The room is engulfed in orange as a ring of fire springs up, hemming them in. She shrinks from the sudden heat, but there is a wall of fire at her back as well.

Why do you think the Hounds of the Heavenly Emperor Mountain ambushed you? Kyubi says. Not just the Hounds, or the Nine-Tailed Foxes, but the whole of the spirit world is waiting to exact their revenge on you.

Hounds of the Heavenly Emperor Mountain? She seems to recall something written by Chao Ying.

Another 350 li west from here is the Heavenly Emperor Mountain. Palm and Nanmu *(楠木) trees grow abundantly on the top, while at the foot of the mountain,* Jian *(菅) grass and* Hui *(蕙) herb grow in abundance. Here, the Hounds of the Heavenly Emperor Mountain dwell. If you rest on a cushion sewn out of their skin, you will be immune to demonic poisons.*

Chao Ying follows her description of the Hounds with summoning instructions. Something begins to dawn on her.

To summon them, add palm, Nanmu, Jian *grass and* Hui *herb in equal measures to a wood stone.*

Immunity to demonic poisons is exactly what the summoning of the Nine-Tailed Fox offers, too.

Very much sought after for the immunity it grants to demonic poisons...

Except the Nine-Tailed Fox is not easy to summon, which makes the Hounds of the Heavenly Emperor Mountain more likely targets for a human summoner. But in order to obtain the same immunity, a cushion of *houndskin* needs to be made. She sways on her feet, not entirely due to the heat, which is increasing in intensity, if that is even possible.

Powerful, ancient spirits are naturally averse to doing the bidding of humans. Many have chosen not to reveal the secret of their summoning.

She turns to the Nine-Tailed Fox. But didn't you ally yourselves with us in order to repel the demons?

Ally? The Nine-Tailed Fox's laughter grates out. We were threatened, more like.

With the Dragon God in command, many elemental spirits gave themselves over to the cause, Master Cloud had said. They did not give themselves over willingly, then.

She closes her eyes and holds the bridge of her nose between thumb and forefinger.

Xue Long stands like a statue carved out of ice.

How does it feel, Ice Dragon? To be at the beck and call of a weak human? Kyubi taunts.

Her blood is bubbling in her veins. All the moisture is being sucked out of her body. She crumples.

Kyubi's eyes flick to her. In that instant, Xue Long dispels the fire. Kyubi turns to him, but Xue Long has already swooped in, catching her in his arms.

Through her half-closed eyelids, she has an impression of sparkling air, afire with myriads of ice crystals.

红尘

Red Dust

22

You are my destiny
A destiny like the fallen snow
My one and only love
You came to me one day like a dream
Walking on sunlit snow
For a moment everything was white
As if my heart had stopped
I love you
I love you
I love you

She hummed under her breath as she worked. She had survived. She would never ask for anything more ever again. She caught Jacq sneaking glances at her a few times, but nothing could dampen her spirits. She even smiled back at Jacq once. There was nothing on earth that could possibly make her happier – except maybe her dreams coming to life.

She had forgotten to check the video of the cube she uploaded, only to find her post deleted for violation of community guidelines. Strange. She had to find time to check what guidelines she had violated.

On her desk sat a bottle of soya sauce that Jolynn had sent her as a reward for spending enough to attain the level of 'Fresh Meat'. She was pleasantly surprised to find the gift in her mailbox, together with a handwritten note: 'The next tier is Rising Star, with Celestial being the final tier. Hope to see you there!' She took it to work with her, where it radiated a wooly warmth. The soya sauce must be of the mass-market, chemically hydrolysed variety rather than fungally fermented, but not even its flat, caustic taste as she soaked her breadsticks in it could dim the pleasure of receiving a gift.

There were always others in the same predicament on Empi. The advice across threads and time boiled down to the same. At the root of the condition of giftlessness was an emptiness in the landscape of gift-bearers. Unfortunately, she could not imagine herself performing the actions required to people this landscape – the very thought of throwing a birthday party filled her with horror. Those who received an abundance of gifts wrote that it really wasn't as great as people might think – more often than not, one got junk. Not to mention the reciprocal effort: the inordinate amount of time spent shopping for gifts on a trip could have been spent enjoying the holiday, for example. They expressed the freedom they felt when they decided to return to an empty landscape.

Empty, from the Old English *ǣmtiġ* – free, idle, unmarried, 'without obligation'. These words could be her description. *Ǣmetta*, free time. Her emptiness, her free time, had been filled with Empi. Her Empi landscape. No birthday parties required. She supposed the soya sauce would be considered a junk gift, since she didn't cook. Takeaways would have provided the condiment in little disposable packets. The only way to eat it was what she was doing now, like dipping cardboard into ink.

She checked how much more she needed to spend in order to reach 'Rising Star'. The gift she would receive in return would most likely be incommensurate, if the sauce was any indicator. But no one had come into her barren landscape before, and she would like to try her hand at watering this relationship. Empi had done a commendable job sending her treats and discounts on her birthdays – save for the year she turned thirty-four, and the fertility clinic had called to offer their special 'Last Chance' package to freeze her eggs, 'clinical consultation and storage for one year' included.

The way the text was arranged on the bottle made it look like it was smiling. She would clean it when she finished the sauce.

Bathing Snow Forest

23

Drink, says a voice from far away.

The icy water clears the clouds in her head a little. She opens her eyes. Xue Long is sitting by her hammock, cradling a cup to her lips.

Don't cry, he says. You'll dehydrate yourself again. You almost became a piece of dried pollack. That Kyubi, he shakes his head, I was already tempering his flame. You could have burnt to a crisp if I'd engaged him headlong.

He touches the cup to her lips again. She drinks a little more.

She falls back into her hammock, groaning. She feels like she's just had a debilitating fever. Every muscle fibre aches. He sits for a while beside her. Finally, he breaks the silence.

I've been thinking, he says. You should learn how to call me.

She opens her eyes and looks at him.

He sighs, as though all the misfortunes of the world have come to weigh upon him.

Like it or not, you have a contract with me, he says. You can call on me.

You have a contract with me, she thinks. What a haughty way of putting it. Not 'I have a contract with you' or even 'we have a contract together'. Of course, 'you are my master' is strictly taboo. She smiles in spite of the pain she is feeling. *Ow!*

Xue Long flicks two fingers against her forehead. Her whole head throbs.

That makes you so happy?

I'm just happy you're finally teaching me something, she retorts.

'Training' turns out to be fishing for sweetfish at Rainbow Lake; at least, she is fishing, and he is reclining against a marbled rock nearby, the very picture of ease and repose. She should have known.

I thought you'd be teaching me how to call on you?

Yes.

That's not what it seems like we're doing right now.

To call on me, you need to cultivate a direct connection. People usually do this by going to places or engaging in conversation with each other. Don't you know this?

No, not really. The Empi meet-ups she had were not what you would call successes.

If that were true, she retorts, shouldn't we doing this *together?*

Ah, but knowing how to catch fish is a useful skill for a disciple to have, won't you agree? As your master, I will not want to deprive my student of the opportunity to practise.

Since she cannot outargue him, she continues fishing in silence. She is quite happy to be here. The lake is called Rainbow Lake because of its clear, variegated waters that change hues depending on the time of day and the angle of perception, with the reflections of the multihued rocks in the area adding even more variances. This must be another one of those places surrounded by a thick spiritual energy that would be nigh on impossible for her to reach by herself. Her heart trills.

The scent of grilled sweetfish soon wafts up from the fire in front of them. Of course, she is the one grilling them and lighting the fire. She'd never before understood why people go to barbeques. She should go hiking or camping more often.

But he won't be there, she thinks, gazing at him sipping his wine. His fingers around the goblet are long and slender. She wonders how it is even possible for fingers to be this perfect. People usually get surgeries on their faces. Looking at him, she thinks a clinic for fingers may become a trend. If only she had a phone in this world, she would post a picture of his fingers on Empi. The breeze seems to have a life of its own, lingering in his hair, making the individual strands rise and fall, like it wants to be near. The light, too, seems to bend, making him the focus of every scene.

After clearing the remains of their barbeque, she unwraps the bandages around his shoulder. Sunlight sparkles on the lake, adding a dose of fire to the jewel-toned waters.

The dark miasma hectoring his wound has mostly dissipated. She tips more medicine onto the cut – the white crystalline powder from his store is supposed to be very effective at neutralising poison.

You're healing well, she says, pleased. You've got a good constitution.

He humphs.

She laughs. She can almost hear his voice in her head, saying, *I've got the best constitution.*

What's so funny now?

She laughs even more. He shakes his head. She notes that he seems to be in good humour.

That day at Kyubi's... she begins casually, but still, she feels his shoulders stiffen. He said everyone in the spirit world is after you. What exactly did you do to them?

He wriggles out from under her grasp, pulling his robes back up over his shoulder. He is wary now, all sense of lull from earlier gone. She finds it interesting, how people like to be clothed whenever they deal with situations. Nakedness always speaks of vulnerability.

Nothing much, he says.

She raises an eyebrow.

I made them tell me the compositions of the stones that would summon them. Some of them I already knew, offered as tokens of allegiance long ago. If I hadn't done that, the demons would have won. You wouldn't be sitting here, questioning me now.

I'm trying to cultivate a direct connection, remember? One of the ways to do this is to engage in conversation, you said. That's what I'm doing now.

Xue Long grumbles something about someone not being so smart when other situations call for it. She waits until he is finished.

All I did was reveal the means by which a meeting with an elemental spirit may be set up. Putting even myself – he looks at her meaningfully – at risk. How the meeting goes is entirely up to them. If the Nine-Tailed Foxes were so unwilling to dabble in the affairs of men, they could have set a more difficult condition for the contract. But all of them asked for an offering of *stuffed beancurd skin with rice*. Did I hold a knife to every one of their throats and ask them to say that?

They must really like *inarizushi*, she murmurs.

If they had asked for human babies, they would not be so popular. They have always been involved with the affairs of humans. Shrines were built to them because of that. They like being venerated as gods. They even married kings and lived in their palaces.

What about the Hounds of the Heavenly Emperor Mountain?

I don't know what they asked for. A contract is an individual thing. They don't have to all ask for the same thing, like the Nine-Tailed Foxes did.

And you? What did you require?

The less you know, the better off you'll be, he says slyly.

And the better off you'll be, she thinks. *So I don't go blabbing your secrets.*

Since the night when they had a run-in with the canine spirits, she has been turning over recent events in her mind. He is so condescending towards the terms set by the Nine-Tailed

Foxes, which means he must think his very clever. After lengthy consideration, the only plausible impossible thing she could have done was to be willing to forfeit her life. She remembers his look of disbelief when she shielded him from the army of hounds. It sounds just like him, to think up a condition like that. *Become my master but be prepared to lose your life in doing so.* She has no way of confirming it, though. Since this is the one thing he will never tell.

She wonders what Xue Long did to make those he bullied reveal the secret compositions of their summoning stones, but this kind of thing is best heard from the victims themselves. She has no doubt she will run into more of them soon. Xue Long is like a lord who has betrayed the confidence of those who had sworn fealty to him. Confident of his powers, having never been in a less than lofty position, he does not know how to feel perturbed by the mutinous feelings that have arisen in the factions of his subjects. But some of the devices against him can prove to be more than mere annoyances and caused him to be caught in her summoning net, snared by a random stone she made.

Ow!

Xue Long has once again flicked her forehead with his fingers.

What's that for?

You've got this calculating look about you. Whatever you're plotting, it won't work.

I'm genuinely worried for you! she protests. How did Kyubi know to find me? Have the hounds escaped already?

I'm not sure. Perhaps.

Who else could have told him, except the hounds who pushed you into the summoning web? They can't get at you, not when you are in your fortress, so they asked Kyubi.

That could have happened, yes.

She looks at him with exasperation.

Relax, he tells her, leaning back on his elbows. I promise to get you back, *every time*.

She lunges at him. He evades her easily. She stumbles on the rocky ground. A hand reaches out and steadies her. She's about to grab him, when she realises the arm is sleeved in red. She looks up in surprise.

The man holding her arm is tall and lithesome. The shining sun brings out the warm reddish tones latent in his long black hair. His eyelashes are unusually long, giving him a slightly feminine appearance. His eyes, looking down at her, are alight with interest.

Looks like my brother is having fun, he says, lips curving into a smile.

Xue Long sees who it is and his eyes narrow.

Chi Long, what are you doing here?

Chi Long? she thinks.

Is this... the *Red Dragon?*

Red Dust

24

Should the end-of-year team bonding be a barbeque?

Her favourite activities were workshops. They were structured, so there would not be empty time for anyone to flounder in. They were also educational. Over the years, she had signed the team up for all sorts of workshops – fermentation, chocolate making, coffee appreciation. Anything that involved food tasting was already halfway to success. In this part of the world, food was a better conversation starter than the weather. If the food had health benefits – like the kefir, kombucha and kimchi they made during the fermentation workshop – all the better. She had hoped the coffee appreciation would put an end to the office's *speciality*. No such luck.

At a barbeque, she would not have the benefit of a conductor orchestrating everything, but it probably would not matter, if she was grilling. She would still be close by, but behind the barbeque pit. Everyone would be grateful that someone was cooking. Should anyone fret she was not eating, she would reply that the cook always got the best bits. Yes, she would suggest a barbeque this year. She always left a blank for 'Any other suggestions?' So far, she had not encountered a counterproposition.

Although her desk was at the entrance of the office, she never looked up when people came in. Nonetheless, newcomers would sometimes try to greet her when they entered. She would look up, slowly, as though her face had been glued to the screen, to give a visible impression of a distinct tearing away from whatever task she had been engaging in at that time – not that it would ever be anything she was absorbed in. Then, she would fix the speaker with a blank stare and say in a completely expressionless voice, 'How may I help you?' Not friendly, but not rude either.

This was what she did reflexively, when a voice greeted her, 'Good morning.' There had been no newcomers recently and the interns had been here long enough to dispense with the formality. She interacted with her co-workers infrequently but this voice was familiar. She looked up and froze. The bangs. The upturned eyes.

It was Brilliant Jade.

The café was white-themed and minimalist, like all cafés that had sprung up all over the island recently. She had suggested they get a drink from a coffee chain, but Ming Yu wanted to check this place out.

'I read they serve really good *tamago sando*, with rhubarb sauce to add a little sweet tartness, and a mayonnaise made of blended tofu and cashew instead of eggs and dairy, so that it won't be too heavy,' she said, parroting what she had heard or read.

An 'ah' was all she could manage in reply. She was still too overwhelmed.

When the egg sandwiches arrived, crustless and cut in neat, dainty triangles, Ming Yu whipped out her phone.

'Shall we take a picture?' she asked.

She nodded. She put on make-up whenever she went to work, so she should look human enough.

Ming Yu held her fingers in a peace sign against her cheek so her face would take on the coveted V-shape in the photo. The phone simulated a shutter sound.

'Another one,' she said, adjusting her head.

She scrolled between the two photos with a critical eye. She did not ask for a retake. Did the photos pass her inspection? Or did she think they would not improve anyway?

'You don't speak much, do you?' Ming Yu said.

'Uh...'

What should she say? To cover her embarrassment, she took a sip of the brew she ordered.

'You look a bit... different. In real life,' Ming Yu commented, hurriedly adding, 'but I can still tell it's you.'

Dismay flooded her body, paralysing her muscles and making it hard for her to breathe, as if her entire being had been botoxed.

The Ming Yu sitting before her was a twenty, twenty-two-year-old woman, not too divergent from her dream-world counterpart, most likely a university student. There were still differences, of course. The Ming Yu who was a student at the Academy of Greatest Learning would never have to hold her fingers in a peace sign against her face. University student Ming Yu's complexion was not bad – she was a young woman after all, considering the lifespan of a human – but there was still a cloudiness like pea soup, with a patch of oily secretion on her forehead produced by even a short walk to the café in the equatorial heat. The academy Ming Yu, on the other hand, had skin the luminous brilliance of jade.

'You look a bit different, too,' she said at last.

'I guess we all do,' Ming Yu agreed. Readily, cheerfully.

Her anxiety ebbed a little. University student Ming Yu was probably a straight talker like her academy counterpart and bore no malice with her comments.

'Guess what happened after you left the academy?'

'What happened?'

'A group of musicians came, seeking students who had summoned an elemental spirit that can sing to join them.'

It was very strange to hear a human voice talking about the academy. Of course, Ming Yu had always been human, even in the other world, but somehow, she had always regarded her as something of a sprite from the dream world. She'd had a presentiment for some time now, a feeling of worlds about to collide.

'One of them is the spitting image of Seung-bin! You remember? From FLWR?'

A rapturous expression appeared on Ming Yu's face, colouring her skin like a red rash.

'Just like you said, I locked myself in the crafting room day and night. Master Zeno wondered what had come over me. I've never worked so hard in my life! Finally, I made a summoning stone I was sure could summon something other than a worm. I would brave a thousand worms for Seung-bin, but still! It was this big—' she made a round shape with thumb and forefinger.

Bigger than the stone she summoned Xue Long with.

'Did you manage to summon a singing elemental spirit with it?'

'A *Lu Shu* (鹿蜀),' she said triumphantly.

'What's that?'

'It looks like a horse with tiger stripes, but with a white head and red tail. If you think that's strange, wait till you hear it sing in a *human voice*.'

She tried, but could not imagine it. Or maybe it was because her brain was already full from processing the fact that Ming Yu was sitting there, in front of her, in a café during lunchtime, eating egg sandwiches and talking about a *Lu Shu* singing with a human voice – and she was *not asleep*.

She felt like she was dreaming, though, and about to be woken up by human voices singing. A long night was about to come to an end, pierced by the spears of light now poised over it. Waiting.

'How are things with your master? When will he let you visit? Surely he has to let you come back for the Novice Trial, right? Are you learning a lot of secrets not taught at the academy?'

The Novice Trial. From another lifetime. She supposed she did not have to pass it now. Nor the evaluation for Summoner.

Crossing Mount Ling Qiu would pose no difficulty for the Ice Dragon.

'...just in case.'

'I'm sorry?'

'I said, I've come to find you. Just in case we miss each other. Since I'll be leaving with my Seung-bin after the Novice Trial.'

'You know, I've been wondering. How did you know to find me? That I exist? I mean, this is amazing, but...'

'Remember the day you came to my room?'

'Yes.'

'You *recognised* my collection. It's not like you know FLWR, but you obviously know what a boy band is. I've invited other people... but it's like they didn't even register what's going on.'

The hum in her ears was getting louder. The other world was approaching. A world filled with human voices and red dust.

'Since then, I've thought about it. Could it be you're not an NPC?'

'NPC?'

'Non-player character.'

'I know what an NPC is. But aren't they something that appears in games?'

'We're in a game.'

Here it was. The collision.

'What?'

'You mean you don't know? Didn't you receive the round black thingy inside a white cube?'

'I did.'

'That's the thing that lets you log into the game. Apparently, we're part of this secret pilot test of a new technology Empi is developing. Do you know the cube opens up at night when you're sleeping? I recorded it.'

She remembered how soundlessly the top half of the cube had split open, how it had levitated. Only a corporation like Empi would have the funds to construct something like that.

'How do you know all this? There's no Empi logo on the disc or on the cube, I checked. And the disc never turned on again.'

'Ah, if you didn't read it in the terms and conditions at the beginning, it's pretty hard to figure out. Since it's stated you're not allowed to post on the Internet, you can't find anything on it. But if you tap on the menu button on the Empi main screen, then tap on "Settings & Privacy", then "Settings", then scroll down until you find "Account", then tap "Settings" again, under the heading called "Account", you'll find "Manage your Empi Account". Tap on that, and under the "Info" tab you'll find this part which says you're part of this beta testing. Tap on it and you'll be able to see the terms and conditions again. You can even turn the device on and off if you don't want to be in the test anymore.'

She was finding it hard to breathe again, like she was drowning.

'Anyway, the day you came into my room, I started to think: what if I'm not the only player in my own mind, like I thought? What if other people also had access to my dreams – or parts of them at least? So I began to search for you. That's when I came across your recruitment for interns.'

'So you came to find me.'

'I did think of sending a message, but what if it's just a recruitment account and you're not the only one using it?'

'That's all right. It's my account.'

'Anyway, because of that, I began talking to other people as well. You know Qing Feng? He's also—'

'Stop,' she said, louder than she had intended. 'I'm sorry, I don't feel too well.'

She got up. The chair scraped across the floor.

'Your coffee—'

She dashed out of the shop.

Light fell all around her, illuminating the night, rupturing it, exposing the snow for what it was – ersatz. Just styrofoam beads. She had probably behaved badly towards Ming Yu and would not be the least bit surprised if she ignored her from now on. So when her phone pinged, she was genuinely taken aback. The message was from Ming Yu: *Are you all right?*

First, she had to look at these terms and conditions. She headed into the mall and, being unable to find an unoccupied bench during lunchtime, stood at one of the standing tables meant for those grab-and-go lunches.

Welcome to Empirean!

Thank you for being part of the pilot test for Project YOUniverse, a revolutionary new gaming experience made possible by the technology of shared dreaming.

As used in these terms and conditions of use ('Terms'), 'Empi', 'we', 'us' or 'our' refer to Empirean Network Technology Co., Ltd., and all of its subsidiaries. Any and all of our Empirean applications, networks, Empirean developer portal, sites and forums are referred to herein as our 'Services'.

YOU ACKNOWLEDGE AND AGREE THAT, BY ACCESSING OR USING OUR SERVICES OR BY DOWNLOADING OR POSTING ANY CONTENT ON OR THROUGH OUR SERVICES, YOU ARE INDICATING THAT YOU HAVE READ, UNDERSTOOD AND AGREED TO BE BOUND BY THESE TERMS. IF YOU DO NOT AGREE TO THESE TERMS, THEN YOU HAVE

NO RIGHT TO ACCESS OR USE OUR SERVICES OR EMPI CONTENT.

Shared dreaming? She had no idea Empi was researching this and applying it to gaming. Games, with their own arbitrary set of rules and non-real-world consequences, have much in common with dreams. When players are immersed in a game, they enter into a state of consciousness akin to lucid dreaming. It was a wonder no one had thought to connect games with dreams sooner. Sculpted by a part of her she had no full consciousness of, her dream was her creation and *not* her creation. She supposed that was how dreams could become games, for their outcomes remain unknowable, their denouement brought about by the initiative of the player, or the dreamer.

The Device

Users gain access to the game world through our Device, which enables shared dreaming.

Automatically Collected Information

- *Your Dream Information. We collect your dream information when you use our Device. This includes information about your activity (including, but not limited to, how you use our Services and how you interact with others using our Services).*
- *Third-Party Information.*
- *Third-Party Providers: When you use third-party services that are integrated with, made available, advertised or linked through our Services, they may provide us with information about you in certain circumstances. For example, when you make a purchase through your EmpiPay, we may use information about your purchase for the purpose of improving your experiences,*

understanding how our Services are being used and customising our Services for you. We may also share information with third-party providers that we partner with to help us operate, provide, improve, understand, customise, support and market our Services.

Advertising Content

- *Empi may include advertising or commercial content. You agree that we may integrate, display and otherwise communicate advertising or commercial content in Empi and, as explained in our Privacy Policy, we may use targeted advertising to try to make advertising more relevant and valuable to you.*

She imagined a city at night, with all its denizens sharing a collective dream. Of course, this revolutionary new gaming experience was all about harvesting data – from dreams, no less, the very thing that fuels the market.

Not for the first time that day, she heard the sound of footsteps, of endless human traffic, trampling on her dreams.

That night, she took the white cube out from her drawer and placed it on her bedside table, positioned her phone so the camera could see the device, and set it to record.

Rainbow Lake

25

I heard you got yourself a cute young master, says the Red Dragon, lifting her chin with a curved finger.

Xue Long says something, but her ears are full of dust, of sand.

Excuse me, she says, to no one in particular. I'm going to sit down.

Both the White Dragon and the Red Dragon stare after her. The Red Dragon makes as if to follow, but Xue Long steps in between them, re-engaging him in conversation.

She finds a relatively flat-topped rock to sit on. How pretty this marmoreal landscape is, with its pale foliations of every colour. The lake shimmers like an infusion of narra wood. But a sandstorm is brewing, a *simoom*, in Arabic – a hot, dry, dust-laden wind and, in Quranic accounts, a type of hellfire – to lay waste to this world, and bury it under ash and sand.

She looks at the two dragons, appearing to be exchanging light, playful banter, if not for the dangerous glint in Xue Long's eyes. How theatrical the pair looks, one in red, one in white. Come to think of it, the pacing of the game is like a drama, too. After the lull of the barbeque, it is now time for some conflict in the appearance of the Red Dragon.

...So the Hounds came to me, saying that if I will aid them in chaining you to the Lightning Pillar, to be struck by lightning for all eternity, they will honour me as the new commander of the spirit realm. They are sorely misguided, of course. I already *am* supreme in the spirit realm. Their participation – or non-participation – is inconsequential. What I'm more interested in is seeing the human who has made you her *servant*. Emphasis on the word 'servant'. Loud guffaws.

I'll be the one to chain *them* to the Lightning Pillar. One bolt will be enough to raze those low-level spirits to ashes. But what makes you think the contract makes me weaker? Sly chuckle.

Am I to believe being bound to that frail human girl makes you stronger? Derisive snort.

Surely, they must have told you how I… *transported* a population of them in order to protect what's mine?

Our contract actually makes him stronger? That's a revelation. The mechanics of the game are clear now that she knows where to look. Mini quests serve as stages you have to clear in order to progress in the game, such as 'Talk to Master Zeno in the Crafting Room' the day she first arrived. Characters that serve as wave after wave of antagonists appear – the Hounds of the Heavenly Emperor Mountain, the Nine-Tailed Fox and, now, the Red Dragon – driving the storyline and revealing more and more plot points along the way.

She is about to be woken up by singing sand. She should lay her heart to rest, before it withers like a flower – a narcissus, caught in an elemental sandstorm. She stands up and walks towards the bickering pair.

Goodbye, she says to Xue Long.

He turns and looks at her. This is the last time she will see that lissome form, *like a dragon riding the clouds*. The phrase is used to describe the goddess in Song Yu's rhymed prose, 'Rhapsody of a Goddess' – about how he meets a goddess in a dream but has no choice but to part, owing to the fact they come from two different worlds.

Not for the first time, she wonders if he cannot be real.

Who is she kidding? In a game, the most taboo thing would be overpowered classes such as his. No, everybody should be human, and dragons some 6* rarity elemental spirit everyone aims to possess, newer additions with each update.

Where are you going? His eyes are still, black pools. She sees herself reflected in their limpid depths. There is nothing behind them. There is only herself. All along.

Over the rope, she wants to say. Offline. Where snow will dissolve, unseasonable, in a land of eternal summer.

But the sands have caught up with her. The songs of the dunes, it is said, are the voices of demons or spirits seeking to lure travellers from the road, in the desert of Lop. They have come to conduct her out of this world, the spirits of the desert. She feels their presences. She spreads her arms and gives herself over to their desert song.

Red Dust

26

The first thing she did when she woke up was to check the recorded footage on her phone. It was just as Ming Yu had said. Once her breathing became regular, thc cube bisected eerily of its own accord, revealing the disc it contained and emitting a blue glow. Empi blue. How obvious everything was in hindsight. The only difference was the tiny red dot that now pulsed at the centre of the disc.

The next thing to do was to shut down the shared dreaming device. Recalling the terms and conditions, she withdrew her consent.

You have been removed from the pilot test for Project YOUniverse.

For someone who sought respite from the endless human traffic in the office, the quietness around her desk could be taken as a refuge, but now the unmitigated stillness seemed almost sepulchral. Snatches of conversation drifted towards her – things that happened at the movie outing she did not go to, what they should get for someone's upcoming birthday, discussions about work she had no understanding of.

So her week passed by in a haze, with not a moment's arrest for her grief. Perhaps there would have been a little allowance for that if she had not distanced herself from hive activities – drunk the coffee from the social stomach, spent her lunch hour with her co-workers. After all, the office lunch hour is the designated time to spill your guts, to seek nourishment from the experiences of another, for the trophallaxis of all that is going on in your life, the effects of which are seldom confined to, but rather linger long after, the hour. In her bid to cut out all harassment from her life, she found herself in a position where she had no one to harass. But she was just sliding around on shifting sand, she knew. What relief would talking to anyone bring? It would just confirm the grittiness of reality.

The morning sun filtering through her curtains on Saturday was still weak, like watery tea, but the oily, treacly sweat secreted in her armpits promised an oppressively hot day. Instead of getting out of bed, she fell back onto it. Her body felt heavy and lethargic, as if she were wearing an iron suit – on a lodestone bed. She had no desire to move at all.

She lay like this until the light was blazing, stray shards escaping the curtains and pricking her eyes. Her phone piped it was time to put food into her body, but just existing from one moment to the next seemed to take up all her energy.

She needed an escape from herself, like her mother when she drank, but there were no spirits in her apartment. *La petite mort* was too short-lived; she was hardly in the right state of mind for the uphill climb and she'd had enough of loving herself. It was a pressing need in her bladder that finally dragged her out of bed.

A sculptor of consummate skill who can only find consummation in his own creation – that is the story of Pygmalion. He never mistakes niveous ivory for flesh, unlike her. It takes a *deus ex machina*, a god from a machine, lowered onto the stage, for his story to have a resolution. Would there ever come a machine that could solve her dilemma? One that could manufacture real live boys from figments, if such a machine was even desirable.

She had gone to bed last night without even removing her make-up. Now her human skin had smeared, revealing what looked like raw fish paste underneath. Her throat was parched and gritty like it was full of sand, but instead of going into the kitchen to get a glass of water, she tumbled back onto her bed and drifted in and out of sleep, dreamless for the first time in ages.

Each time a hot wind blew, sunlight would shine through the parted curtains like an orange floodlight, bouncing off the walls, ceiling and glazed tile flooring in all directions so it felt like she was trapped inside a giant piece of amber. Her body was coated with a gluey sweat, although inside she was racked with a raging thirst. Still, she did not feel like doing anything at all.

Finally, she could sleep no longer. The sun had long gone, but the stifling heat remained. With great difficulty, she pushed herself up and stumbled into the kitchen, drinking from the spout of the kettle. She felt groggy and light-headed, like she had slept out for a whole day in the desert. When she returned to her room, she found the air was rank with a faintly ferrous and sulphurous odour. Her sheets, in particular, were damp and gave off a smell like a mixture of fish sauce and soured milk.

She should not have slept so much during the day. Melancholia is always worse at night. She launched Empi and began streaming *Love in the Snow*. The way to silence one's stream of consciousness is to supplant it with a stream of digital consciousness. She could not muster her full attention and so could not become fully invested in the drama unfolding on the screen, but the actors did fill the emptiness of the night, like two-dimensional standees in the chamber of her mind. Josie Wong was, of course, pure pixels. As for Park Min-jae, pixels were all she ever saw of him anyway. The world had become flat once more, a handscroll.

She continued scrolling after the episode came to an end, finding comfort in the lighted square of the screen, the modern hearth. Her curtains began to lighten. She felt pinpricks of pain in her eyes, as if there was sand in them. When she blinked, her eyelids scraped across her corneas. She tossed her phone aside and closed her eyes, scratching her scalp, which only made the itching worse, like insectphora crawling all over. Ashy flakes fell on her pillow like dust. Her scalp seemed slathered with a layer of oily butter.

She felt a queasiness in her stomach and realised she had not eaten anything since the unfinished coffee she had with Ming Yu. There was only a half-eaten Mars bar forgotten at the back of her fridge that had absorbed the smells of all her previous takeouts. The bricky candy bar reignited her thirst. The kettle was empty, so she went to the sink and drank from the tap.

Another sweltering day. She wondered if she should not consider installing an air conditioner in her bedroom. Her mother had not installed air-conditioning owing to the rise in bills it would entail. The clouds of dust and dirt that would be generated in a furnished flat as a result of installing an air conditioner meant it would most likely remain an unrealised project. Nevertheless, she began half-heartedly swiping through air-conditioning options, until she checked her bank statements and realised that she had spent, in the last few months, what it had taken her years to save. She rubbed her eyes and pain coruscated over her eyeballs. Not a dream, then. It was never a dream when she wanted it to be, always a dream when she wished it to be real. The numbers on the screen were implacable, final. She lay motionless, as if the slightest movement could hurt her. Here she was, shorn of love and money. She felt raw, peeled open, emptied. Yet, she could not even complain of having been swindled or seduced. Where was the lover? The cheat?

When she next woke up, the fish glue on her body had fermented like liquamen from viscera in the sun. Her mouth had also seemed to become a fermentation vat for the sugar she had consumed. Her tongue, especially, felt coated with slime.

A ravenous hunger gnawed at her. She placed an order for kimchi ramen, with a message to leave the food outside 'if I am not back yet, as I am going out'. She waited five minutes after the doorbell rang before stepping out to collect her food, but still she met the old lady living in the unit across, standing by her gate.

'I thought you're not coming out to take your food,' she said with a gap-toothed grin.

She smiled at the space beside the old woman and scuttled back quickly into her own apartment. She liked this shop because it served radish kimchi, which makes a good summer side dish, in addition to the more common cabbage kimchi. The only problem was the addition of kimchi-flavoured vapours to the mixture of organic volatiles in her stuffy apartment.

The noodles sat inertly in her stomach, causing her to feel a postprandial somnolence. She lay on her bed, like a snake digesting its food. Her neck felt as if there was a piece of wood wedged in it. *Smartphones – Pain in the Neck? 5 Tips to Alleviate Neck Pain Caused by Smartphones. Your Mobile Phone May Be Destroying Your Eyes. BRAZIL – Woman Develops Acute Glaucoma From Drama Binging. Fatal Attraction – Your Video Game Marathon Can Kill You. Man, 23, Dies in Internet Café in Taiwan's Third Game-Related Death of the Year.*

These people all collapsed suddenly, she observed, from things like heart failure, exhaustion, dehydration, as though they had been out in the wilderness and not on a chair. So absorbed, they did not even realise they had run their bodies ragged. In contrast, ingesting pills, wrist slitting or leaping off a high-rise required more courage.

She had just eaten. Slept a lot. For good measure, she did the exercises from *Don't Get off Your Couch: 5 Exercises You Can Do From Your Sofa*, pedalling her legs in the air like an overturned beetle.

She dozed, woke up and dozed again. At 4am, she was wide awake: the time of wakefulness for lovers, the broken-hearted and the screen addict. She was badly in need of a shower before going to work. Now was as good a time as any, if she did not want to be late.

A three-day-old stench hit her when she removed her underwear, which was covered with a half-dried glutinous paste like curdled milk. Here, things were always putrefying, unlike the bacterialess, phosphorescent cyberworld. Her body, soft and wobbly, was the colour of suet. Veins near the surface of her skin on her upper thighs and below the knee joints reminded her of vinaceous worms. She averted her eyes and scrubbed herself – perhaps harder than necessary, for liver blotches appeared on her skin. She gave her teeth, furfuraceous when prodded with her tongue, a good brushing. She blow-dried her hair thoroughly. She never understood people with wet hair on the train – it reminded her of wet octopuses.

The early morning train was only half-full. She was a whole hour early for work. She switched on the lights and wandered around the workstations of her creative colleagues. She was seldom in this early, if ever. Had there been others around, she would never have found the courage to be there, but no one had anything pressing to do that necessitated an early start to the day, after wrapping the holographic installation project. She recognised a miniature replica of Michelangelo's *David* on an unidentified character modeller's desk and what looked like one of Turner's aurous landscapes on Jacq's. Did the designers of her dreamscape also have such pictures attached to the walls of their desks? She remembered how the mountainous terrain surrounding the academy reminded her of Fan Kuan's *Travellers Among Mountains and Streams*. There was a birthday card standing on Jacq's desk, half-opened in the shape of a V, like a vertically resting butterfly – on its right wing were the words, 'Happy birthday to my love, Nick.' Since when had her colleagues been dating? She suddenly realised how little she knew of them. They were little more than cardboard characters to her.

Midweek, she received an email.

Dear Summoner,

Do you have anything to tell us about your experience in the pilot test for Project YOUniverse? Are you interested in an exclusive behind-the-scenes peek into the developmental process? Join us on EmpiLive and stand a chance to win rewards that will give you a head start when the game officially launches!

After work that day, she found herself in the cool glass lobby of Empi's regional headquarters, naturally lit by filtered sunlight. Every megacorp needs its tower, and Empi was no exception. She might have seen the headquarters many times against the skyline, but this was the first time she had actually been inside. The building, with its iconic façade of creepers and flowering plants, had been featured in numerous architecture magazines. Solar panels covered the roof, taking advantage of the abundance of sun in the tropics. A biodiesel plant in the building generated electricity using oil collected from the eateries. The soaring vertical garden, which she had seen often in online articles, stretched from one end of the lobby to the other, containing plants adapted for a dry, cool Mediterranean climate. She took a deep breath. According to a video, the air was kept richly oxygenated by the indoor plants, as well as the oxygenators in the air-handling units. Even when the annual haze blanketed the region, air purifiers maintained indoor air quality. A harvesting system that collected rainwater, as well as condensation, from the air-conditioning units ensured all the plants were completely self-irrigating. The water collected was also used to flush the toilets. She rode the elevators, which were powered by the electricity generated from the kinetic energy produced by the lift car itself. The shapes of the furniture were simple and geometric, in shades of oat and eggshell, which she found infinitely easier on the eyes than white minimalism, although the chief consideration was probably to make anything in Empi blue pop. She sat on a couch. Contrary to its luxurious appearance, it was uncomfortably soft, which made her feel like she was sinking into quicksand.

She dined in one of the publicly accessible cafeterias. Employees ate for free. Only organic ingredients were used, with no artificial flavour enhancers. Food costs amounted to millions of dollars a year for the company – she knew from the PR put out. No corporation would provide their employees with organic meals, balanced by a nutritionist, for free, without saying a word about it.

On Friday night, she attended the livestream for the simplest reason: she wanted to talk to someone about what she had been through. That the someone happened to be the developer was incidental.

'What's your idea of utopia?' began the moderator from the development team. He had on a pair of kitten ears that kept swivelling around, as did his female colleague.

'The term was coined by Thomas More from the Greek, meaning "no place", which is very much preferable to words like "paradise", don't you think? *Paradeisos* means "garden" in Greek. Rather than an Eden or peach blossom spring to which we yearn to return, utopia is a product of human society, something we can create. Project YOUniverse is the apotheosis of this dream.

'Imagine a world with *you* at its centre. The sun shines for you and the stars glow for you. Modern life is such that people seldom feel regarded, isn't it? There's just one problem. When you are surrounded by you, it can feel like a gilded cage. Shared dreaming provides a solution by harnessing the subconscious: the gaze of an alterity, even if only illusionary, freeing you from the prison of yourself.'

'Yet, the subconscious is not so easily harnessed,' interjected the lady. 'In our earlier tests, the world was simply overtaken by the libidinal desires of the participants. We're in the territory of the subconscious, and the alien guests we've invited overpowered the ego.'

The things the pair said were incredible. But the kitten ears lent an air of drollery to the entire proceedings.

Stickers with eyebrows raised or wiggling, giggling or guffawing, appeared.

'Now, now. Get your minds out of the gutter. We pulled everyone out before it could go there, recalibrated the shared dreaming device, and sent it out to more participants who would be a good fit for this world, according to our data. At one point, it almost seemed like an impossible task to regulate the subconsciousness. No two minds are the same. What works for one person may not work for another. But the prize is a map of the *terra incognita* of the mind. So we pushed on.

'The last round of testing was a resounding success. It could be the participants were uncommonly disposed to dreaming, more unresisting to suggestion, less attached to reality or more comfortable with the idea of having multiple selves than most. Whatever the reason, their trajectories through the world were the most coherent. Not only that, they produced a stabilising effect on all the other dreamers with them, just like how our realities are validated by others around us. After analysing the brain patterns from the last test, we are able to replicate the effects and the final version of the shared dreaming device can now be born. Thanks to all of you.'

They were making her feel like a messiah of some sort, but she wasn't so sure she had helped to liberate the world.

'Everyone acted out their own stories. Yet, a small percentage withdrew from the test and didn't come back. We checked our data, nothing seemed to be wrong. If you withdrew and you're here in this livestream, we'd be very grateful if you'd just take a few seconds to tell us how we can do better.'

There was a moment of silence as the moderators read the replies.

No time to sleep.

Stuck in a place for too long.

Can't get the elemental spirit I want.

She supposed it could seem baffling. A cause for concern, even, if players who seemed to have everything going for them wanted to leave. It suggested there was something imperfect about the world, that it was not enough. It mattered not to her that the dragon was clockwork, but clockwork dragons cannot love you back. Insofar as love is the acknowledgement of the Other, there was no Other to acknowledge. But how could she explain that to these two, or anyone for that matter?

There's nothing wrong with the world, she typed at last. *Only, what I wanted can't be found in it.*

What she wanted was a genesis of the soul.

*

The crimson sunflowers on the windowsill had long wilted. There was hardly any space for her existence in the living room, crowded with her shopping. She had been wrong. These were not objects. They were commodities. Objects speak of objections she could push against. She bought them to weigh down her dreams. Commodities, products of the dream machine, are commodious but empty. She ran a finger along her purchases. They were distinctly powdered with a layer of dust.

She hauled the merchandise to the lift. The void deck, usually empty unless there was a wedding or a wake, filled up as though the refuse from an offshore landfill was returning to haunt the city's doorsteps. Conducting a wake would not be a bad idea, actually. She had just woken from a long dream. These items would be a cairn to the life of sorts that had come to end in the dream world.

She made herself remove her make-up and dragged herself to the shower, even though she felt like just flopping down on the floor. The acne on her face had worsened and the inflammation showed up even through her green concealer, prompting her to be more diligent in her cleansing regime. Perhaps one day, automatic showers – like automatic car washes, but for human bodies – would become the norm for households. The human being collapses upon a heated porcelain slab and is conducted into the shower stall, where the scrubbers and sprinklers get to work.

On her bed, she realised several prototypes of her idea already existed, taking the incarnations of tubs, seats and cubicles fitted with jets, rollers, robotic arms. Truly, there is nothing new under the blue-lit sun. A video concept even surpassed what she had dreamed, featuring a chair with shower and breakfast-making functions that could transform into a bed and had wheels to convey the sitter wherever they wanted to go. She gorged herself on trifles, noting with irony that one of the treatments for computer game addiction was something called 'wilderness therapy', which involved immersing the addict in a natural environment in a group, in order to develop their social skills outside of a game.

As she had grown up in a city-state, wildernesses meant nothing to her. Perhaps owing to what she saw and read before she went to bed, she dreamt she was a drab-coloured bird pecking at concrete, trying to reach the soil for worms. It was the first dream she'd had all week, or the first one she could recall having when she woke up. If dreams make reality seem dull, then shared dreaming makes even dreams drab. Or maybe she had just lost the ability.

It is the mundanely coloured creatures that are naturally selected and populate the earth.

*

She was at her favourite Nanjing restaurant, with the soymilk porridge she always ordered in front of her, and the date she had been assigned by the customer service officer at the agency. He had dressed in white, like she had specified. He did not question her when he asked what she liked or disliked.

She had a craving for the soymilk porridge in the afternoon but did not feel like going alone. She first asked Ming Yu – after apologising to her – but she preferred having pancakes instead. After promising her she would have pancakes with her another day – it was uncertain, of course, when Ming Yu would feel like having pancakes again – she found Marc, who was assured to be a wonderful conversationalist, guaranteed to make her lunch an enjoyable experience, and would leave after an hour and a half.

'So, if you are good-looking, there's this whole slew of idioms in Chinese to describe you, all involving dragons. You may, for example, be dragon-browed – *long mei feng mu* (龙眉凤目)' – here the straight brows of a certain dragon came to her mind – 'or have the bearing of a dragon in expressions such as *feng biao long zi* (凤表龙姿), *feng gu long zi* (凤骨龙姿) or *long zi feng cai* (龙姿凤采). Or I may say you are like a dragon steed – *long ju feng chu* (龙驹凤雏). Of course, that's a horse, not a dragon, but even the best horse is described in terms of a dragon – you get the picture?'

Marc nodded, his expression that of rapt attention.

'The thing is – no one has ever seen a dragon before, so the entire language is based on something nonexistent.' A dream, basically.

That is, until shared dreaming lets you see without sight. Some things, when touched by the light required by vision, would turn to smoke and scatter like ashes in the wind, like ghosts who fail to shelter under umbrellas upon sunrise.

'If you're good at speaking, your speech is like a dragon in flight – *long teng bao bian* (龙腾豹变). An extraordinary talent may be compared to a leaping dragon – *long yue feng ming* (龙跃凤鸣). To compliment someone's spry dance moves or calligraphy, you tell them *jiao ruo jing long* (矫若惊龙) – "you move like a dragon".'

If Marc thought she was bizarre, he gave no sign of it. His intent gaze never left her face. She could almost hear the silent words of the script: *be interested to be interesting.* He was a brilliant role-player in their role-playing game.

'So a good-looking person is like a dragon, an eloquent person is like a dragon, a talented person is like a dragon and a graceful person is also like a dragon. If this dragon were a real person, he would be quite incredible, wouldn't he?'

It had occurred to her that she might never be able to escape from the dragon's clutches. How could she, when everything reminded her of him? He was there everywhere she turned, unless she could wipe off her face, rub out her history, cast all the words she knew into oblivion – undo herself, basically.

Marc produced a pack of cards and, at his suggestion, they played a game where the loser got flicked on the forehead. What fun they had. They could be heard even from the next table.

'Let's stop here,' she said finally.

Her forehead was sore.

'We could do something else. There's still time.'

'It's okay.'

An expression of unease passed momentarily over his face.

'Don't worry. I enjoyed myself. I just want to go home now.'

He searched her face and found no hint of displeasure. The calm returned to his demeanour. In fact, this was a good thing.

'Then I hope we'll get to work together again,' he said, reaching out for a handshake.

She took his hand, wondering if they were taught to do that at the agency. Wouldn't it be better for business to draw as little attention to the charade as possible? Yet it was because he was a professional that she could prattle on about dragons to him without fear of rejection.

'Yes, goodbye.'

She flitted from one role to the next – an employee worthy of her salary, a colleague who did her job but whom no one knew very much about, a neighbour one could live with, a friend hovering just on the edges of orbit. Anything more would require too much time and energy.

She was an actor who could not immerse herself on stage. As a result, all her roles were of little interest. She twisted her body, donned the costume and tried to imitate the facial expressions, but all she succeeded in doing was looking unsightly and unnatural. She envied the others for their innate talents, the strength in their bodies, the ardour in their spirits, but she was an old branch tossed among flowers, cut off from the earth, no longer able to bloom no matter how hard she tried.

Be careful what you wish for. Didn't she wish for her dreams to become flesh? They did. Just not in the way she'd hoped. They made it through the front door of her office in the form of paper, plastic, polystyrene. The snow-bathed forest – is Xue Long still there, sleeping? Nourished on the dreams of other players? – now adorned the wall at the entrance as a framed poster, next to Aria's. Another luminous entry to the studio's portfolio. *Let Your Legend Begin.* Life is filled with astral alignments. It turned out Verge was responsible for the concept art for Project YOUniverse, now officially *Spirit Summoners.* Every leaf, every frond, was designed in-house. The lake of rainbows where she fished with Xue Long. The verandah she sat upon with Brilliant Jade. She wasn't that far off with Fan Kuan's *Travellers Among Mountains and Streams* after all. The invoice had been processed by someone else, but she found digital library subscriptions by the concept art department for high-resolution images. There they were. The snakes coming out of the ears of beasts and gods. Arrayed in the paintings of Jiang Ying Gao (蒋应镐) from the Ming dynasty. Was there no end to the patter of feet? Trampling on the desolate plain of her heart?

She was tempted to get the Xue Long plushie, although this *kawaii* version with its neotenous features meant to inspire love bore no resemblance to the Xue Long she knew. Was it a coincidence the word for piteous is *kawaiso*, as used by Lady Murasaki in *The Tale of Genji* to describe helpless women arousing compassion in men? Plush doll women.

Elemental spirits overran the city, appearing on clothes and schoolbags, home décor and kitchenware. She managed to stay away from the live-action movie, the drama series, the stage production, the web novels and comics, the theme park – although her colleagues were always discussing Spirit Summoners and all its spin-offs. There were seldom meetings in the conference rooms when she got off work now, or unconscious people on the couch when she came in. Most left on time with her, sometimes even earlier. *How Shared Dreaming Changed Expectations of Work More Than Any Virus. Is the Dream of Work-Life Balance Finally Here Due to a Game?* She thought the sclerite masks of her colleagues looked even more stupefied than before, but Empi maintained that their tests showed no evidence of any adverse impacts of shared dreaming on sleep. *Shared Dreaming a 'Healthy and Normal' Part of Sleep According to Empi's Researchers.* In fact, a chronically sleep-deprived generation was getting more shut-eye, which was a good thing.

In the dream world, Jacq had become a summoner with quite a following, it seemed. Famed for not only her exploits but also her beauty, she lived with her aquatic, pearl and jade-laying elemental spirit, a *Ru Pi* (絮魮) – shaped like an upturned teapot, with the head of a bird but tail and fins of a fish, its cries like chiming stones – next to the source of Deluge Waters in the Mountain-Where-Birds-And-Mice-Nest, in conjugal bliss with Nick. They had been planning to get married for some time, but things were considerably more burdensome in real life. The summoning world called her Lady Pearl Jade, because she always arrived on expeditions wearing trailing robes woven with the gems.

Alex's accomplishments were no less congratulatory. He had gained a minor reputation for his creative approaches on expeditions. In fact, he was recognised as a Summoner after completing an SSS-ranked expedition, but not in the way expected. A rich man had put up half his fortune for anyone who helped him to ride the vulpine, horn-backed *Cheng Huang* (乘黄). It is said whoever gets on its back will live for 2000 years. Instead of summoning the elemental spirit, Alex created a play through which the man might live for more. She had never heard him mention his animated film since. Gone also were Jacq's plaid and tartan, the pleats that had to be ironed. Sometimes she even came to work in the sweatshirt she wore the day before. In her imaginings she would tell them.

I was called the Dragon Summoner, she wanted to say. *Back then. You weren't there.*

She could almost see him, whenever her co-workers talked. His eyes would be starved, searching, piercing the dimensions with his gaze. Where are you? he would say. We can be together again.

She could only wait; time would be held in suspension, a strange, sad note stuck on a broken record, for her soul to trickle back into her body, breath held, not daring to blink, lest his mirage disappeared.

Sometimes she wondered what she was resisting for. No one else seemed to be having any problems, barring isolated cases like *Not Enough for Rent, but Forks Out Five-Figure Sum for Life-Sized Spirit Summoner's Figure*. The problem was not the game, but the player, right? All she had to do was turn on the shared dreaming device. She could do that from the menu on her phone. She could not count the number of nights she had spent in the blue glow of the cube, trying to warm herself in its heatless light, but she could no more bring herself to discard it than she could carve out her entrails, or cleave her soul from her body.

She had taken up ceramics after watching videos of vessels of all kinds of shapes and sizes flowering on the wheel under the potter's hands, seemingly unfettered by gravity. There was something hypnotic about the spinning wheel and a certain satisfaction to be had from wrestling against intractable material. Some days, she forgot herself and hunched in a position for too long, and felt nerves and muscles screaming when she stirred. She would look up and wonder where the slice of time between the hands of the clock had vanished. In water and sand, the wordless thoughts that passed through her were recorded. The vessel on the wheel was a clay tabulation of all her movements – from the most delicate of touches to the firmest pressures – containing the memory of her wrestling against her own body and against gravity, her castle in the air in a languageless space, where she may seek refuge from words.

She was on her way to a ceramics exhibition – a fellow hobbyist from the studio had suggested a group of them attend together – when her bus was caught in the slow-moving traffic along the expressway. She snacked surreptitiously on a cheese cracker to elude the bus captain's attention. The cheese cracker proclaimed itself to be real three times on the bag, wearing high-tops and a baseball cap. She took it for its word and bought it without checking the ingredients. Now she finally did, she discovered it was indeed made with cheddar, in addition to Yellow 5 Lake, Yellow 6 Lake and Blue 1 Lake.

Watching the river of cars winding along at snail's pace, she understood why the chronicler of the *Book of the Later Han* described a seemingly never-ending line of carriages as flowing water and interminable horses as a rippling dragon, which later evolved into the expressions *che shui ma long* (车水马龙) and its permutations. Long covered in concrete, the dust no longer flies. Digital traffic does not stir up any dust. Perhaps humanity does not end up as dust, as much as pixels – digital footprints harvested and resurrected as a digital avatar when the organic matter disintegrates. The trees rose on both sides of the hilly slopes flanking the multi-laned road like the covering of a massive animal, evoking visions of crouching dragons and tigers lying in wait – *long quan hu wo* (龙跧虎卧). The earth is the dragon's flesh, the rocks its bones, the vegetation its hair.

She leant her head against the window and watched the interview for the umpteenth time. Taking place in what looked like a meeting room at the company's headquarters in Shenzhen, viewers were given the impression they were peering into a slice of a day in the developer's life. To further this impression of spontaneity, the interviewer was dressed in a fashionably casual way, as though he had just dropped in from the street. The developer was in a red-checkered shirt and ripped jeans – comfortable clothes to go to work in, and a fortuitous splash of colour against a neutral background.

Interviewer: Ever wished to be able to live out your own fantasy? Now you can, in Empi's MOST REVOLUTIONARY *game of all time,* Spirit Summoners. *We're privileged to have Wang Zhe (王哲), head of the development team, here to have a chat with us.*

Wang Zhe: Hello! It's a pleasure to have this chance to talk about the game with everyone. The development team has worked very hard on it. We hope it continues to get lots of love from all of you.

Interviewer: Spirit Summoners *is a game that does not take up your waking hours at all, as it takes place when you are sleeping. Since its introduction, shared dreaming has gained widespread application, but it was first developed for gaming purposes. Can you tell us more about how shared dreaming is used in the game?*

Wang Zhe: Yes, shared dreaming's applications stem from its ability to simulate reality. As such, it came to be used in areas where the re-creation of hypothetical situations would be beneficial, such as in emergency drills and skills training. This opens up boundless possibilities when it comes to recreation. In gaming, an endlessly open world is created by the player, as open as the mind itself. Of course, in order for the world to

be a safe environment where people will actually like to play, there are limits as to what you can do or you will face negative consequences as a result of your actions, as in real life. You may get yourself killed or be rebuffed by the characters. But, ultimately, it is a world where you will be able to realise all your fantasies, so look forward to it.
Interviewer: Wow, I can't wait to immerse myself in it already!

Once again, she thought: *Perhaps it is not machines that want to cage humanity in a prison of simulated reality, but we willingly build the cage ourselves.* The number of real friends mattered less than the number on display. What the trip was really like was less important than how it looked when collaged on the screen, with all the intervening time excised, the way we experience time in fiction. Everyone's holidays looked exactly the same, as though chosen from a set of options – the same bubble tea, the same bowl of noodles, the same swing in Bali. Right down to the angle of the shots from the best photo spot indicated by the signage on the site or found by numerous travel bloggers before.

Cocooned on her bed with EmpiStream – those were all the elements she needed for her to retreat into herself. The question of the man dreaming he was a butterfly, unsure upon waking if this world was real or if he was a butterfly dreaming he was a man, was no longer of interest. What concerned her was not which world was real, but how she could be sustained within her cocoon. To a caterpillar, the cocoon is its home, no matter where it is attached. Thus encased, suspended in a state of inanimation halfway between adult and child – that was what the world demanded of her anyway, never mind if she would never be able to fly. Unfortunately, she could not prevent ageing. Since sunlight causes photoageing, hiding inside her cocoon could be more practical than flying in the fields.

People feel kindlier towards the young. The other day, she walked past a domestic worker pacing the void deck carrying her employer's baby. The young woman was smiling and planting kisses on the gurgling child's face. It struck her, how tenderly the woman was treating an infant not her own, compared to her impressions of the carers gathering at the void deck with elderly charges. In those instances, they would sit on the staircase, conversing in their native tongues, while the elderly men sat in their wheelchairs parked a few metres away. The old men did not speak to each other. She could almost see the chrysalises of silence around them like physical things.

Interviewer: Ever since Spirit Summoners *became a worldwide phenomenon, several players have physically got married to holograms of NPCs in the game, making* Spirit Summoners *the most popular media out of which cross-dimensional marriages have sprung. Did you expect the game to have such an impact on players?*
Wang Zhe: I actually received an invitation to witness the online ceremony of a player marrying Master Xiao Chen, from the Academy of Greatest Learning, as sort of like a 'father' to the bride. Unfortunately, I was unable to attend and a member of the team who came up with her character design went instead. How shall I put it... I'm cheering for the player to overcome obstacles in his pursuit of happiness, including dimensional barriers. But I also hope someone from the same dimension will turn up eventually... I heard the company producing the hologram also receives requests from people who suffer from PTSD, the disabled and the elderly, who think the product may be helpful and a source of comfort to them.

She noticed the developer did not answer the question directly, which was understandable, as no developer would want to be accused of encouraging such behaviour. Yet, he could not be entirely unsympathetic, as these feelings of attachment towards the characters were exactly what sustained the game. He also quickly directed the attention of the viewers to sections of the society in need of support, using the vague term 'helpful' and stopping short of any definitive curative claims.

The first time she watched the video, she searched for the company called GateTablet that produced the horizonal tablets with the holograms floating above them. It called to mind the spirit tablets used in ghost weddings, orientated flat instead of upright, earthen vessels that manifest the spirit – or virtual character – in the real world. Some recordings of the weddings were available online. The officiality they had in common struck her, as if to make up for the yawning gap left by the insubstantial bride or bridegroom.

She was surprised when Master Dawn appeared on screen with a completely different face, speaking with a babyish voice and hiding her mouth behind her hands when she smiled. The blue robes were still the same, although the plain, practical material had been changed to something gossamer and diaphanous, embroidered with stars like the night sky. It must have cost the player a couple of thousands of dollars to get the outfit modelled, just like a wedding dress. She should have known everybody's impression of affability would be different. She had tuned in thinking it would be like seeing the wedding of a friend – one that had been there her whole life, in fragments of a character in a book or a movie, and whose origin had become indistinct. She may encounter her one day, or she may never cross actual paths with her. But when she does, she will recognise her immediately, or at least part of her, because she has known her all along. This version in the video, however, was not one she recognised. It prepared her for the other weddings that followed.

Abandoning the East Asian aesthetic of the game, one player's groom – her elemental spirit – was dapperly suited in a tuxedo. Personally, she felt it was a bit out of character, but that might be exactly what the player was aiming for – to rebel against his character settings. The jewel on her ring was a replica of her summoning stone. She walked in wearing it because there could not be an exchange of rings. Her honeymoon took place when she went to bed that night – somewhere exceedingly dreamy, without a doubt. Another player had decided to go on a honeymoon in the real world, taking her GateTablet along. She could have carried him in her luggage but she chose to book two seats on the plane – anything to make him take up more space.

At the 14:31 mark, the interview came to an end. The interviewer and the developer said their farewells, and the screen transitioned seamlessly – or in a way she had become accustomed to, so the seams ceased to be noticeable – to images of mist and moonlight making up the opening sequence for the trailer of the game:

Empirean Dream Entertainment presents

About the Author

Pan Huiting lives and works in Singapore. After studying Fine Art at Nanyang Technological University, Singapore, she completed a Master of Arts in Singapore and a Master of Research in Fine Art at the Royal College of Art, London. Huiting has taught courses in global art and art criticism at Nanyang Technological University, and has displayed her art in exhibitions across Singapore and London. *Red Dust, White Snow* is her debut novel.